REIGN

A BWWM ROMANCE

YASAUNI

Reign

Copyright 2019 by Yasauni

Published by Mz. Lady P Presents

All rights reserved

This book is a work of fiction. Names, characters, places, and incidents either are the product of the author's imagination or are used fictitiously and are not to be construed as real. Any resemblance to actual persons, living or dead, business establishments, events, or locales or, is entirely coincidental.

No portion of this book may be used or reproduced in any manner whatsoever without writer permission except in the case of brief quotations embodied in critical articles and reviews.

ACKNOWLEDGMENTS

First, I want to thank God because without him I don't know where I would be. I would like to thank my mother, Debra. Y'all don't even know the shit my mama go through with me and these books, I'll get off work at two in the morning write until four, then call my mom and ask her how it sounds. She has truly been a real trooper with me, and when I'm too tired to run back and forth for her, she's understanding about it sometimes lol.

Mz. Lady P. (Suge), you're a great publisher and thank you for not dropping me when I work your nerves, and thanks for not dropping me when I quit writing and quit the company, etc... lmao. I quit a lot, and you never give up on me. You always there when I need you, and I appreciate it for real.

I have to thank my Auntie Bilhah, She and my mom are my biggest fans and best supporters.

To the dream team that makes up Mz. Lady P Presents, I love y'all.

To my friend Tina, man you have become more like a sister. Many people have gone left on me, or we just don't talk to me because of my crazy work schedule, but you keep up with me around my schedule. You are always sound reasoning in my life and with my books. I love you.

I can't forget the best test readers in the world, Lakeitha Chatman and Shaniece McWilliams.

I know I'm probably missing a lot of people, but never charge it to my heart. I love all y'all, and to my readers, I have to give y'all a huge thank you!

CONNECT WITH ME

Facebook: Yasauni Mc
　Instagram: Sauni
　Twitter: Yasauni McWilliams@sauniD

I dedicate this book to the McWilliams family. I love all y'all ugly ass, lol. We have our ups and downs, but no matter what, we are rocking with each other.

SYNOPSIS

Synopsis

Losing her mother at a time in her life when young girls needed them most, Reign Davis felt that her world had ended. Shaking off her hurt and pain, she decided to lean on the things her mother instilled in her. Coming from a world filled with poverty and pain in, holding yet concealing the pain of losing her mother, Reign decided to excel beyond the statistics the world classify her as.

REIGN

"Reign, get up. It's time for school." I rolled over closing my eyes tighter, not ready for the day I have ahead of me. "Reign, I know you heard me."

My mother had opened the door to the bedroom that was just big enough to fit the twin-sized bed and the small chest of drawers that sat in the corner.

I opened my eyes glancing at my mother before sitting up, moving slightly to the right to make sure that I didn't cut my leg on the spring that was sticking out of the side of the mattress.

"I'm up," I stated before standing up and going over to the window getting the clothes that had been hand washed the previous night.

"You're okay?" my mother asked me with wide glassy eyes.

I looked at her knowing she was as high as a plane on autopilot. She looked a little pale around the eyes as if she wasn't feeling well, but I decided not to acknowledge it because she wouldn't tell me the truth anyway.

"I'm tired, ma. I tossed and turned all night long because the springs are starting to cut through the middle of the bed. Can I just take the day off?" I asked my mother, hoping that she would see the bags under my eyes and give me just this one day.

"No. I bend over backwards every day just to make sure you have what you need. I know what I have to offer you is not the best of life, but it's more than a lot of people have. All I ask is that you go to school and get an education. Reign, you haven't made it this far by taking days off just for fun, and you're not going to start now. I know I can't afford to put the high prices shoes and clothes on your feet and back, but I have given you the best of what I have to offer you, and that's a mind to do the right thing."

I stood there looking at my mother as tears pooled up in her eyes. She quickly turned her back to me stopping and turning back to face me.

"I'll get you some more blankets to make a pallet over the bed." She turned and walked out of the room. Not soon after, I heard the door to the one-bedroom apartment close.

I hurried and pulled out the iron plugging it up and placing it on the floor at the head of the bed. I grabbed the old, rusty, steel chair from the corner sitting down looking out the window watching my mother cross the street to the nearest drug dealer as I place the hot iron on my pants. I ran to the bathroom, showered, and threw on my uniform.

I looked at the time, and I was running a little late, so I ran top speed down the stairs and directly into my mother. She wore a huge grin on her face as she slightly bit down nervously on her bottom lip, all signs of her being high.

"Hurry up Reign so that you won't miss the bus." My mother grabbed me by my arm and rushed with me to the nearest bus stop.

"I love you, girl. Have a good day at school." My mother kissed me on my cheek.

"I love you too, ma," I replied, stepping on the bus getting my mind and body ready for the two-hour ride I have ahead of me to get to Northside College Prep High School.

* * *

"Ms. Davis, do you mind answering my question?" I jerked my head up drowsily looking at the board wrecking my brain trying to recall what the instructor was teaching.

"Um..."

"Mr. Love, I need to speak to Reign Davis. It's important," my principal walked in the room at the perfect time. I looked between Mr. Love and my principal then back at Mr. Love.

"No, go right ahead," Mr. Love responded as I grabbed my book bag and hurried to the door.

"Reign, listen. We need to get to Mount Sinai Hospital. Something is wrong with your mother."

My mind began to race I took off running right behind Mr. Montgomery to his car. I had been in this high school for four years and every teacher in here knew my situation and knew my mother, Queenie. They knew she was a drug addict that did her very best for her child. There hasn't been a time that my teachers would say they needed to meet with her, and she didn't show up whether she was high or sober.

"Did the person that called say what was wrong with her?" I asked Mr. Montgomery as he weaved through traffic.

From the look on his face and the speed that he was going, I knew it wasn't good. I sent up a small prayer for the only person that I had in the world as we pulled up to the hospital in record time.

"Queenie Davis room please?" I said to the nurse breathlessly. She gave me a brief, sad expression and cleared her throat before speaking.

"This way please." She walked us to the elevator.

I locked my fingers together and began twisting them to calm the ball of nerves that sat in my stomach as we took the short ride to the third floor. There my mother was lying in bed looking like death was lingering at her bedside. Her caramel skin looked so pale, and the smile she wore this morning was a look of anguish. I walked over to the bed, and she gave me a weak smile. Tears filled my eyes and threatened to run down my face.

"I told them not to bother you while you were in school." My mother weakly raised her hand to my face instantly wiping my tears like she had done so many times before.

"Ma, what happened to you?" I asked.

"Just listen to me, baby. I'm not going to make it."

"No don't say that. You're going to be ok," I was trying to encourage her as well as myself.

"Listen, as I told you earlier, I've done the best that I can with you, but I've always known that you were destined for greatness." She grabbed my hand and gave it a weak squeeze. "I gave you the name Reign because I knew no matter what came your way, you would be able to conquer and reign over it all. You got this, baby. You will make me happy no matter what."

I got in the bed with my mom and laid there going into a comforting sleep until the doctors came rushing in pulling me out of bed in a rush. Mr. Montgomery jumped up pulling me back into his arms. As doctors worked on my mom, I stood there watching them until they called her time of death. I turned and looked at Mr. Montgomery knowing I had no one left in this world. I picked up my bag and walked out of the room, Mr. Montgomery was right behind me.

"I'm so sorry for your loss, Reign."

"I want to go home."

I walked out of the hospital with my mind racing and my heart in pieces. Queenie may not have been what people considered the perfect mother, but she was mine, and she was the perfect mother for me.

We pulled up to my house in no time, and I thanked Mr. Montgomery and let him know I would see him in school tomorrow. I walked to the apartment going to the kitchen to get some water. On the old wobbly table was a letter from Harvard. With shaking hands, I opened the letter. I read the first words in the letter and began crying. My mother wouldn't be here to see me off to Harvard. I had gotten in, and her dedication is what got me there. I cried as I held the letter close to my chest and walked into my room lying on the newly padded bed. If nothing else, I knew that my mother loved me unconditionally. She just had a habit that she couldn't run away from.

. . .

THREE YEARS Later

"Reign, wake up babe. You're crying in your sleep." I was lightly shaken out of my sleep, and I felt warm hands caressing my face. I opened my eyes realizing that I wasn't in the one-bedroom apartment that I shared with my mom.

"I'm ok, Blake," I said groggily sitting up looking around the room.

"Are you okay, Reign?" Blake asked, looking at me with concerned brown eyes. He pulled me up in front of him wrapping his arms around me. I buried my face into his chest taking a deep breath and inhaling his freshly showered smell. His huge frame engulfed me, and I felt content for the moment. I eventually removed myself from his embrace.

"I'm fine, Blake." I stood on my toes and gave him a swift kiss on the cheek.

Blake sat on my bed and watched me intensely as I gathered my clothes. He walked up behind me wrapping his arms around my waist, kissing the back of my neck. I exhaled loud before stepping out of his reach.

"I need to shower so that we won't be late." I quickly grabbed my towel and walked out of the room.

Once I got to the bathroom, I locked the door and leaned against it. Blake and I had been together for about four months now. He was the epitome of what every girl on campus wanted in a man. He was six feet tall, had perfectly tanned skin, dark brown hair that he wore messily, had a body to die for, with a handsome boyish face. His frat brothers referred to him as Babyface, but when he was on the ice playing hockey, everyone called him Destruction. To put the icing on all of that sexy cake he had what we in Chicago like to call swag and a fat bank account to match. Blake had what the people on campus referred to as old money. His grandfather was some type of oil tycoon.

Coming from the type of background I'm from, you'd think that would be enough to light some type of spark under me for him, but it wasn't. Blake was a cool person. He helped me out whenever I needed anything, and I didn't even have to ask for it. It started with him giving me a thousand dollars here and there. At first, I wouldn't even accept his help, but he always found a way to give me what he wanted me to have.

The first time I noticed him one year ago, I was working a shift at Denton Bar and Grill. He saw me by the bathroom with my coworker and roommate, and I was crying because I didn't know how I was going to pay my portion of the rent. As she tried to console me, Blake had walked by.

Once I got myself under control, I went to wait my tables. Blake was in my section. Once he and his friends got ready to leave, he handed me his receipt for eighty-five dollars and twenty-three cents with a thousand dollar tip. After looking at the small piece of paper, I caught him at the door.

"I'm sorry. You wrote the wrong amount on the receipt. Let me print you another one up. Give me one second. He looked at my nametag.

"That won't be a problem, Reign. It wasn't a mistake. I knew exactly what I was doing. Thank you for your excellent service." He went to walk out of the door.

"I really appreciate it, but this is way too much. Please let me print you another receipt." I had grabbed him by the arm stopping him from leaving. Blake gave me a small smile, and I dropped my hands from his arm.

"I actually don't feel like it's enough, so if you print another receipt this time, I may leave three thousand instead." He smiled at me knowing that he was about to get his way.

"Thank you so much, and you have a good night," I said to him feeling defeated. Blake turned and walked away. I hadn't seen him at the bar again, but about two semesters later, we both ended up in the same business class.

As I said before, he was everything that any woman would want in a man. He is attentive and goes out of his way to show me that I'm special to him, but I didn't know if I wanted to take things to the next level with him. He was the perfect guy to be with. I just wasn't sure if he was the perfect guy for me.

I came back into my room fully dressed for class. I grabbed my bag, and we left the house. Stepping into the spring air, we walked hand and hand towards the campus.

"Do you work this weekend?" he asked me, pulling me out of my thoughts.

"No, what do you have in mind?" I asked him not really wanting to know what he had planned for us. I took this weekend off to sit in my apartment alone and eat several pints of cookie dough ice cream.

"I know that this Saturday coming up is the anniversary of your mother's death, and I don't want you in the house sulking, so how about you come home with me and meet my folks?"

I stopped walking as he looked at me expectantly. Meeting his folks was taking our relationship to another level.

"I really don't know about this, Blake," the words stumbled out of my mouth.

"Come on, Reign. I'm going home for the weekend, and it would be best for both of us if you came with me. If I had known what this weekend was for you before I made these plans, I would have pushed them back." As he continued to talk, the thought came to my mind.

"Wait, how did you find out that this Saturday was the day that my mom died? I don't recall telling you that?" My hands were on my hips, my right eyebrow was twitching, and I was feeling the need to explode right there.

"Reign, don't get upset, but Amber was worried about you, and she told me. She said that sometimes at night she would hear you calling out for your mother in your sleep. She was only trying to help," he said reaching his hands out towards me. I quickly stepped out of his reach.

"That BITCH!" I yelled out watching Blake's face turn red before I stomped away from him. He quickly caught up to me grabbing me by the hand.

"Don't be mad, Reign. Please calm down. We just want to help you. I know I can't replace your mother or the hurt that you have gone through, but I can try to help make this day a lot easier for you. Just come with me this weekend, please."

I know some people may think that I'm overreacting, but I'm a private person. The only people on this campus that knew what went on with my mother was Amber and one of the instructors that I met when Mr. Montgomery dropped me off almost three years ago. This situation is so crazy to me. In a couple of months, I will be twenty-one years old and the same pain of the day I lost my mother still haunts me as if I'm still that seventeen-year-old kid.

"Don't cry, please."

Tears threatened to fall from my eyes and Blake quickly kissed my eyelids. I exhaled a breath that I was holding in.

"Ok, Blake I'll go with you."

* * *

I SAT in class anxious for it to be over, I had agreed to go with Blake, but I still had to handle this situation with Amber. As soon as class was over, I grabbed an Uber to the Bar and Grill. I walked in, and Amber was the first person I saw, so I walked towards her grabbing her hand pulling her to the back.

"We have a couple of things to discuss. First roommate, rule number one don't ever let Blake into our apartment or my room without my knowledge. Second, don't ever in your life tell anyone anything that I tell you in confidence. I confided in you about Queenie, and the first thing you do is tell Blake," I raised my voice, and Amber's beautiful, high yellow skin tone went crimson within seconds.

"I was just trying to help, Reign. For the last three weeks, you have been calling out and crying in your sleep, and I didn't know what to do. That was the only reason I let Blake in the house this morning. I didn't mean anything by it." Amber looked in my face

"Did he do something to you? I will kill him with my bare hands." Amber started slipping her jogging pants over the shorts that were a part of our uniform.

"Calm down, Amber. It's nothing like that, but I do feel like telling Blake was something I needed to do myself. I know you were only trying to help, but please don't tell anyone else my personal business."

Amber nodded her head like a child that was being disciplined and started taking her jogging pants back off. I shook my head as I changed into the light blue fitted crop top and black shorts that could barely hide my butt. I laughed at the thought of Amber's five feet five and one hundred ten pounds running up to Blake trying to fight. It would be like me trying to fight him. Amber and I were about the same height I was probably about fifteen pounds heavier, but who could ask for a better friend. She thought I had been hurt and was ready to get pinned down for me. Unfortunately, the type of pain I dealt with no one could take it away, so I could only hope that time would make it better.

BRENTON

I woke up to the smell of burning bacon and my head pounding. I begin checking my surroundings as I didn't have a clue as to where I was. I sat up in the bed looking around just as the blonde beauty walked in the room carrying a tray to the bed with a smile on her face.

"I'm happy to see that you're awake." She sat the tray right in front of me, and I smiled.

"Thank you."

I searched her face trying to figure out what the hell happened last night. I began to dig in the food that I desperately needed and flashes of the previous night started coming back to me. I was at club Mix It Up getting plastered in VIP when she showed up. *What is her name? What is her name? Damn, I think I'm getting a little too old to still be waking up to random females that I didn't remember ever coming home with.*

"You like it?"

I nodded my head trying to hold down the food while praying I didn't get food poisoning from this half cooked/ overcooked meal. The grits were stuck together like she glued them to the fork, the eggs were scorched, the biscuits were so raw that if I poked it, I would hear the Pillsbury Doughboy giggling, and let's not forget the charcoal she considered bacon. I gave up on trying to eat the food and drank the orange juice that was sitting on the tray.

I jumped up out the bed frantically running through the room looking for the bathroom. I opened the door to what I assumed was the bathroom. I looked around, but I couldn't hold it in anymore. I emptied the contents of my stomach right there in the closet. I turned to look at the woman with tears in her eyes sitting on the bed.

"I'm so sorry, Brittany. I will pay for everything I destroyed plus more."

Although I didn't feel it was my fault, I would have a fit if someone did to me what I just did to her. On second thought that wouldn't have happened to me because I know I can't cook.

How does a person mess up on squeezing oranges? I could've sworn I drank the orange peels instead of actual juice.

"My name is Kelly, asshole," she said, getting up and going into what is more than likely the bathroom locking the door.

"I'm sorry, Kelly," I said before pulling a huge towel that was in the top of her closet and cleaning up my mess before leaving her house. When I got in my car, I called my lawyer gave him the address of the house I just left and told him to send a check there for twenty grand.

I took the short drive to my house pulling up ten minutes later. I had an hour to get ready for a meeting. Walking in the house and going into the kitchen, I grabbed a glass filling it with tomato juice and emptying the contents of the glass on the way to my bedroom. I went to the closet pulled out a black suit then went to the shower.

* * *

EXACTLY AN HOUR LATER, I walked into my office handing my receptionist the address to Kelly's house.

"Please send flowers to her with a card that says I'm sorry for the inconvenience." Brenda nodded her head and handed me my messages.

"You have a meeting in ten minutes," she said while wiping a piece of lint off my jacket.

"I know thanks a lot," I replied before kissing her cheek.

Brenda was an older lady that fussed over me like I was the son that she never had. I had hired her three years ago after I made the choice to have a personal meeting with my last receptionist that ended with her bent over my desk. I dropped all of my things on the desk getting a much-needed cup of coffee and made my way to my meeting.

I sat in the meeting barely listening to a word that was being said. My head was pounding. I had to stop partying in the middle of the week. My body was giving me signals that I'm getting a little too old for this lifestyle. A couple of years back I could party all night then make it to work acting like I had slept comfortably for eight hours. I stood up in the middle of one of my employee's presentation.

"We have to cut this meeting short. I'll have Brenda to email you the exact date, but I'm thinking in about three weeks. I'm sorry for any inconveniences!" I walked out of the boardroom before anyone could say anything. Going to my office, Brenda stood up handing me some aspirin and a glass of water.

"I swear you should be my wife. You know what's wrong with me without me having to say anything. You're the best." She smiled at me.

"This isn't for the hangover you walked in the door with, and this is for the migraine that you're going to have after dealing with who's in your office." I glared at Brenda. She ignored my glare and turned on her short-heeled shoes walking away. I stared at her back for a few minutes before taking a deep breath and walking into my office.

"Mom."

My mother was standing with her back to me looking out the window. She turned around smiling at me with her arms open to hug me. I walked over into her warm embrace.

"And dad." My back stiffened at the sound of his voice.

"Hello, Andrew." I walked away from my mother and sat behind my desk.

"Benny, don't you think this act of yours is getting a little tired?" my dad questioned me smugly. I picked up the pen on my desk and began twirling it between my fingers.

"My name is Brenton. No one has called me Benny in over twelve years, and I wish you would stop trying to bring the nickname back. It's over just like our relationship." I slammed my hand down on the desk then stood up to pace the floor.

I couldn't stand my father, and the term blood is thicker than water is a false statement when it comes to him. I think I would rather put my safety and trust in someone I have never met before then to be in the same room with Andrew. He made my blood boil just by breathing the same air as I did.

"I am your father. You have my last name and my blood running through your veins, and even a blood transfusion couldn't change that." He stood up to face me.

"And as usual you are wrong. We may share the same blood, but my surname is Prescott, that name belongs to my grandfather, not you."

My father and I were in a standoff at this point our matching multicolored kaleidoscope eyes angrily staring each other down unblinkingly. I felt like this was my company that we were standing in, and I wasn't planning to lose this battle. In Andrew's house, or should I say my mother's house, I would have to respect their wishes or leave. He came uninvited to my office. Therefore, he needed to respect my place of business or leave.

"Please, you both need to stop. Andrew, you promised you wouldn't do this," my mother said looking between her husband and me.

"Brenton, I know that you're still angry with your dad and maybe some of the blame of what happened should fall on me, but your grandfather needs you."

"So, why didn't he just call me?" I kept my glare on my father while talking to my mother.

"Because I wanted to see you," my mother answered the question sounding defeated.

"I'm sorry, mom." I walked away from my dad's challenging glare to embrace my mother in a hug.

"You know our yearly gala is coming up and your grandfather wants you there," My mother stated.

"Let him know I'll be there." Kissing my mother on the forehead, I stepped away from her and sat back down behind my desk. My mother turned to my dad, grabbing his hand.

"Let's go Andrew, and I love you, Benny." I looked at my mother.

"I love you too!" I opened my laptop getting ready to do some much-needed work. Before my parents walked out of the office, my dad turned to me.

"You should try to find a date and make sure it's someone intelligent. We all know the type of easy, bimbo women you like."

"I guess I am my father's son," I replied quickly.

"Andrew, bring your ass on," my mother told my dad in a tone so demanding that you heard a hint of her southern twang. I laughed at my mother. She was finally putting my dad in his place. I think I might enjoy this gala.

To say my father and I had stranded relationship would be an understatement. My mother and father had separated when I was about six years old. You would think with him having a good woman like my mom by his side that she would be all that he wanted and needed. He helped run my maternal grandfather's multi-billion dollar company, and my mother waited on him hand and foot, but her love couldn't keep my father's penis where it belonged. I had to be about five or six years old when my mother and I had gone to his office for a surprise lunch on the first day of my summer break. We walked into the room that they held their daily morning meeting and there was my father on top of the junior vice president humping her like a dog in heat as she moaned out his name.

The basket of food that my mom was holding in her hand crashed to the floor. I will never forget how all of the blood drained from my mother's face, and she went pale. My father was so into what he was doing that he didn't even know we were standing at the door until the blonde head lady tapped him on his shoulder and pointed at my mother and me. At that point, my mother turned me back towards the door pushing me out of it. I heard my mom yelling you're fired, and the blonde lady ran past me naked as the day she was born with her clothes in her hand. I stood right at the door as I heard things being thrown around the room and crashing down to the floor. My grandfather came to the door grabbing me by the hand and leading me to his office.

That night when my grandfather dropped me off at home, my mother was lying in bed and she stayed that way for days, maybe even weeks. That summer I stayed with my grandfather until my mother was able to get herself together. My father came by the house twice a year to see me, and that was my birthday and Christmas. Although my mother and father had gotten back together years later, my father and I still hadn't been able to rebuild the relationship that we had when I was five. I still couldn't understand how he could just leave and only come to see me twice a year. As I got older other, things just seemed to push us further apart until we ended up where we are now.

I closed my laptop. Between the hangover and the migraine that was caused by my dad, I wasn't getting any work done today. I took off my suit jacket and tie and opened up the top buttons of my shirt.

"Brenda, I'm gone for the rest of the day," I said as I walked past her desk she held up her hand with two more aspirin.

"You're the best, Brenda. See you tomorrow."

I walked out of the building I needed a drink and the best place for that was Denton Bar and Grill. I hadn't been there in a couple of years, but it was time that I pay my friend and business partner a visit.

"Welcome to Denton's Bar and Grill. I'm your waitress, Reign. Can I start you off with something to drink?"

She set the menu down on the table with a manicured hand. My eyes roamed over her body as I sat there stuck admiring her beauty. She was perfect. Her cocoa, silky smooth skin and doe-shaped brown eyes had me enthralled. Her black, thick natural hair hung past her shoulders in a mass of curls that seemed soft to touch. She had to be about five feet five inches tall, and she looked small and delicate almost innocent. I let my eyes roam over her again. She was kind of top heavy to be so little with a waist that tiny.

"I'm going to give you a couple of minutes, and I'll get back to you, ok."

I was still dumbstruck, so I nodded my head slowly until she turned to walk away and that did it for me— her round hips and plump behind practically spilled out of her shorts. I sat at the table feeling like a teenage boy that had talked to his high school crush for the first time instead of a grown man that runs a multimillion-dollar company. Reign walked back over to my table with a smile on her face and a glass of water.

"What can I get you, sir?" My mouth instantly went dry from her smile. I took a sip of water before responding.

"Your number?" I questioned more so than stated.

"I'm sorry, sir. That's not on the menu. Would you like something to drink besides water?" Her smart remark threw me off.

"Yes, you." She frowned her face in the cutest way.

"I'm not on the menu either. Please, excuse me."

Reign walked away, and I could tell she was pissed off. I couldn't wait to see what happened next. I wasn't used to being rejected, so this was new to me. Women usually looked into my bluish-green eyes and fell right into my trap. If that didn't work, my platinum cufflinks and twenty thousand dollar Cartier watch that I wore would catch their eye, and they would do whatever I wanted just for a shopping spree. I could tell Reign would be different, but I was up for the challenge.

I sat at my table concentrating on the menu when a shadow towered over me.

"You haven't come to the bar and grill for years, and now you're here harassing my employees?"

"You shouldn't have put them in such appealing uniforms," I responded without looking up.

"Those uniforms were your idea, remember?"

My eyebrows furrowed together trying to remember as Dennis sat down across from me laughing, sitting a pitcher of beer on the table. I poured myself a mug and drank the entire thing before responding to my longtime friend.

"Yes, I remember now. We need to change those things. I can't come in here and see her in those every time I visit."

"Well, just stay away for another year and a half and you won't have to worry about it," Dennis slyly remarked.

I sat up in my chair looking across the room at the woman that was playing hard to get. I always thought of myself as a man that loved women regardless of race, color, or creed, but Reign was alluring. I could only imagine the way she would taste and the sound of her voice moaning my name while I was giving her an orgasm of a lifetime.

"Did you hear anything I said to you, Brenton?" Dennis was snapping his fingers in front of my face.

"What did you say?" I finally acknowledged.

"I said leave Reign alone. She's a good girl paying her way through business school at Harvard. She doesn't need everything that comes along with dealing with you."

"And what is that supposed to mean?" I studied Dennis as he leaned over the table with a grim expression.

"You know exactly what I mean, Brenton. You're my best friend, and you have never talked to a woman and didn't have an ulterior motive. Mainly you are trying to love them and leave them or should I say, fuck them and leave them. Reign is not that type. She's just trying to do better for herself and mind her business while doing it."

I sat staring at my longtime friend trying to figure out if I was really as bad as he was saying. I personally didn't think of myself that way. I felt more like I was giving women the time of their lives in a timely fashion. It wasn't my fault that most of them didn't interest me in any way after a night of making passionate love.

"I have to get back to work, but remember what I said." Dennis stood up to walk away from the table. He walked up to Reign, saying something to her before going to the back. Reign walked back over to the table plastering a smile on her face. I could tell she wasn't happy to be back at my table, so I made it easier for her.

"I would like to order a basket of hot wings with blue cheese, please." She wrote my order down.

"Can I get you another pitcher of beer with that?"

Her sensual voice had me lusting for her, and the way she licked her lips before putting the top to the pen to her lips, I envisioned her wrapping her mouth around my long hard cock and making my knees buckle from her firm grip and wet mouth. My penis pulsated and stirred to life as I thought of her wrapping her legs around me as I stroked into her deep. I shifted in my chair a little.

"Yes," I finally answered her question and watched her hips sway as she walked away from me. I had to find a way to get Reign in my bed, but for once in my life, I just didn't know exactly where to start.

REIGN

As Blake and I pulled up to the massive house that he considered home, I sat in the front seat of his Bentley Continental GT Coupe wringing my fingers. Blake reached out placing a hand over mines.

"You have nothing to be nervous for. They're going to love you." He pulled my hand up to his lips and kissed the palm of my hand. I pulled my hand down and gave him a smile that showed more courage than I was feeling at the time.

"Let's do this," he said, and I responded by opening the door and sliding out the car.

The front door to the house opened, and a middle-aged woman stood in the door smiling at both of us. I turned back to look at Blake as a man dressed in a black suit walked passed us getting the keys from Blake and pulling out our bags.

"Mom," Blake said as he went up the stairs into her waiting open arms. I walked up the stairs slowly behind him. Blake held out a hand to me, and his mother gave me a smile that melted away all the nervousness I felt.

"Mom, this is my friend Reign. Reign, this is my mother, Julie Prescott." I smiled.

"Nice to meet you, Mrs. Prescott." I held out my right hand to shake hers, and she pulled me into a hug.

"Nice to meet you too, Reign." She let me go stepping back taking another look at me.

"You are beautiful, darling," she said with a hint of southern drawl smiling at me again.

"Thank you, Mrs. Prescott," I said as she pulled me in the house by my hand leaving Blake behind us.

"No thanks needed, and please call me Julie."

I nodded my head at her as she led me into a sitting room that was bigger than the entire apartment that I shared with Amber. Julie pulled me down on the expensive huge white leather couch next to her.

"So tell me how did you and Blake meet?"

I began to tell her about the day that Blake came into my job and how he left me such a generous tip. I also told her how we didn't see each other after that until we ended up in the same class. I ended our discussion with how Blake and I became friends. She listened attentively nodding her head, but really never said anything for a minute.

"Well Ms. Reign, it's time to get ready for lunch. I'm sure you two are starving. Follow me. Yours and Blake suite should be ready by now." I stopped walking causing her to stop and turn back to look at me.

"Blake and I don't have to share a suite. I would prefer to sleep alone." Julie gave me a puzzled look.

"You don't have to be modest, dear. I won't pretend that you guys don't share a bed on campus." My eyes widened.

"We don't, and I wouldn't feel comfortable." His mother smiled at me.

"Since the other rooms aren't ready can you guys just share the room for the night, and I will have a suite ready for you by morning, or I can have Blake sleep in the sitting room for the night."

I was still a little nervous, but I couldn't impose on Blake and take over his room like that.

"I can't put him out of his room like that. It will be fine for the night, but I will really appreciate my own room tomorrow." She showed me to the room that I would be sharing with Blake.

"We'll meet in the dining area in about an hour. I'm sure my husband can't wait to meet you." I smiled at her as she closed the door to the room.

I hurried going through my bags trying to find something to wear to lunch before meeting Mr. Prescott. I'm sure with all the elegance of the home I would need to wear something better than jeans and a baby tee. I began to pull things out of my bag throwing them on the bed when Blake walked in.

"What are you doing?" I stopped going through the bag long enough to look up at him.

"I'm looking for something suitable to wear to lunch." Blake laughed at me.

"Jeans and a shirt is fine, Reign. We may be wealthy, but we're still human. You don't have to go all out. It's just lunch. We're only eating food." I exhaled.

"Okay."

"Go and get showered and I will find something for you to throw on."

I grabbed everything I would need for my shower and went into the bathroom knowing I had about twenty minutes to get myself together. Once I had gotten out the shower after drying off, I walked into an empty room. I looked on the bed, and Blake had taken out my black jeans with my white baby tee that had *"Black Girls Rock"* on it with a beautiful black girl on it with huge Afro puffs and red lipstick on. I looked at the time noticing that I didn't have time to look through the walk-in closet that was big enough for a king size bed to fit in it. I shrugged my shoulders. Putting the outfit on ran my fingers through my thick loose hair and went to find the dining room.

As I walked to the bottom of the stairs, Blake was standing there waiting.

"I love that shirt." I smiled at him as he grabbed my hand leading me to the dining room.

When we walked in there the conversation between Mr. Prescott and Julie instantly ended. Mr. Prescott stood looking me over before he gave me a tight smile.

"You must be Reign?" His eyes ran over me once more giving me a slight chill.

"Yes, how are you?" I lifted my hand to shake his, and he stared at it impassively and sat back down in his chair.

"Do you think your outfit is appropriate due to the occasion?" I looked down at my outfit.

"I thought it was okay for a casual lunch," I responded, rolling my eyes before I could stop myself.

"Actually the shirt she's wearing was my idea," Blake stated before his dad said anything else. Blake pulled out my chair for me to sit at the table before his mother cleared her throat.

"I was just telling Andrew how you two met and…"

"And I felt that the move that Blake pulled would attract the type of person I feel you are." Julie cut her eyes at her husband.

"Andrew, that's enough." Mr. Prescott stood up from the table.

"I'm no longer hungry." Julie rolled her eyes as he walked away with an attitude.

"Don't mind him, Reign. Let's just eat lunch and afterwards you, and I can have some girl time and leave the men here to do whatever it is they do."

I nodded my head at her, but all I wanted to do was go back home. This weekend was supposed to be one filled with fun and good memories so that I can have something good to remember on this day, but at this point, all I could do was think about how Queenie would have handled his rude behavior. I sat and went through the motions of eating lunch, I wasn't really hungry, and after eating a good meal, I wasn't quite full either. All I wanted to do was ball up in the bed and sleep the entire weekend until it was time to go home.

"Are you ready to go out, Reign?" Julie had opened the door to the room without knocking to see me lying in bed. I sat up a little acknowledging her presence.

"No, I'm really not feeling up to it, but thank you." I turned my back to the door, and after about a minute, I heard the door close.

I closed my eyes as tears ran across my face onto the pillow. I felt alone and singled out, it times like this that I missed my mother the most. Before I knew it, Morpheus had taken over, and I fell into a deep sleep.

* * *

I WOKE UP LOOKING AROUND. I had to collect my thoughts and soon remembered I was in Blake's room. Although the door to the room was closed, I could hear yelling but couldn't make out what was being said. I got out the bed walking over to the door cracking it just a little.

"This is what your son spends our hard earned money on?"

"What the hell are you talking about, Andrew?"

"You know exactly what I'm talking about, your son wasting our money on this girl. He could've at least found one with class."

"What is that supposed to mean? She's a good girl with a bright future ahead of her."

"Her plans for the future is swindling our son out of his inheritance, and I won't stand behind him or you with that gold digger." I begin to walk closer to where the voices were coming from.

"You just can't be happy that Blake has found someone that he felt he could bring home and have a nice weekend with his family. You always feel that anyone he brings around us has an ulterior motive. I really don't understand where you pulled this from. You took one look at the poor girl and bam she's a gold digger. What the hell is wrong with you?" Julie paced back and forth while talking then stopped to look at her husband waiting on an answer.

"There's nothing wrong with me, Julie. Evidently, I'm the only one within this house that's thinking clearly. This girl has never had a damn thing in her life. She made it to Harvard on a wing and prayer. My son is more than a great catch for her; he's a meal ticket. She comes from a broken home with a mother that died from a drug overdose. Christ, he gave her a thousand dollar tip the first day they met, so what else do you think she could want from him?"

I turned around and made my way back to the room just as quietly as I had walked up on their conversation. I wonder was all this going on because I was poor or if Mr. Prescott just didn't like me because of the other obvious reason. I walked in the room pulled out my phone and texted Blake. Before he texted back, I pulled out an outfit walked to the bathroom to take another shower before dinner.

This weekend was turning out to be worse than I thought it would, and this is the reason I stayed in the house for my mom's death anniversary. That was the worst day of my life, and if anything felt worse than that, I didn't ever want to find out what it was. This weekend was definitely close to that because I was starting to feel that I was losing myself in this house with Blake's racist father.

I came out of the shower to find Blake stretched out over the bed.

"You know you look good in your towel." He looked back at me and stood up looking at me as if he was ready to pounce. He stood in front of me, and the smell of liquor hits me so strong that I instantly became dizzy.

"You're drunk Blake, just lay down." I took a step back away from him.

"Why?" He asked, stepping directly in front of me snatching my towel down, looking at my body, and licking his lips.

"Please don't do this, Blake." I barely recognized my voice as it came out in a soft whisper. I tried to bend down and grab my towel while keeping my eyes on him, but he put his foot on it and went to lounge for me. I turned trying to run back to the bathroom, but Blake reached out quickly catching me. He snaked his arm around my waist pulling me back.

"Let me go, Blake." I got a louder as he threw me to the bed stretching my arms over my head. I could hear my heart thudding in my ears as I tried to kick at him. I needed to get him off me, and now my adrenaline kicked in high gear as I tried to fight to keep my innocence.

"My dad said you would try to fight, but it's ok. With all the money I have given you over these couple of months, I have paid enough to do whatever I want to you."

"Blake, this is not like you. You're drunk, please!" I pled as he took his tongue down my ear to my neck.

"Your begging is turning me on. Say it again," he mocked me.

I struggled under him as he held me down with one hand and began to unbuckle his belt. When I heard the zipper on his pants, come down and he fumbled to pull out his package while moving my legs apart with his knees. Out of nowhere, I thought of the only thing that I hadn't done. My survival instincts kicked in high gear scream my brain relayed the message to my mouth.

"HELP!!!! HELP ME!!" I continued to yell at the top of my lungs.

Blake brought his mouth down to mines trying to cover up my screams. I yelled louder, and when his mouth went to cover mine, I closed my mouth embedding my teeth into his lower lip. I held on to it until he released my hands coming to his knees. I sat up kicking at him trying to get out the bed when his hand came crashing hard across my left cheek.

"You BITCH!" he yelled lunging back towards me.

I let out a piercing scream and kicked at him finally landing my foot exactly at what I had been aiming at. He yelled at the top of his lungs rolling off me onto the floor. Julie ran into the room opening the door with Andrew quick on her heels.

"What the hell is going on?" Julie asked with a look of shock on her face Andrew stood behind her with a smirk on his face running his eyes up and down my body. I didn't say a word just got off the bed as Blake was pointing at me holding his package. I stood over him lifting my foot in the air stomping down on Blake's nuts so hard that I thought I heard them crack. Blake yelled out one more time. I quickly grabbed my clothes throwing on the first thing I could find in the bag.

"What's going on here?" Andrew asked me trying to stop me from walking out the door.

"Ask that fuck boy on the floor," I stated, walking out of the bedroom door. Julie ran to me with her eyes wide once she realized what was actually going on.

"Reign, I'm so sorry baby. I never thought my son would do anything like this to any woman." I didn't say anything to her as I went down the stairs. I had to get out of here. Once I got to the first floor, Julie grabbed my hand.

"Please Reign, just wait. Where are you going to go? How are you getting home from here? If you want you can stay the night on the other wing of the house, and I will take you home tomorrow." I turned to look at her like she'd lost her mind.

"Julie, your son tried to rape me, and you want me to spend the night under the same roof of an attempted rapist, not to mention the fact that as soon as your husband saw me naked, he looked at me like a hungry wolf circling a lamb? You have been very nice to me I really appreciate it, but I will walk back to school before I stay another night under this roof." I opened the front door walking out.

"Wait, Reign," Julie grabbed my arm again. "let me pay for you a cab. Just give me five minutes."

I walked away from the door. I had my own money and could pay for my own cab. The door opened back up.

"Reign, I don't know what my wife was out here saying to you or trying to do for you, but personally I don't feel sorry for you. You people walk around and feel that you can tease men like me and think nothing is supposed to come from it."

"You people? So, you feel it's okay for your son to take advantage of me because I'm a black woman?"

"No, I feel that my son has given you more than enough money to take what he deserves. It has nothing to do with you being black, but it has everything to do with you being a money hungry whore."

I had to admit that I was appalled by his words. I thought it was because I was black, but it was because I was a woman. Andrew grabbed my arm I pulled away getting defensive.

"If you touch me again, I will do worse to you then I did to your son." He quickly dropped his hand from my arm stepping back. He went in his pocket pulling out a piece of paper.

"I figure two grand will get you where you need to go." He held out a check.

I turned walking away from him. I had entertained him way too long.

"Two grand doesn't pay for silence."

I began to take that long walk to the end of their driveway. I could hear Mrs. Prescott faintly calling my name for me to come back. I increased my pace hoping she wouldn't follow after me. Once I was outside the gates of their property, I stopped taking several deep breaths trying not to break down. A couple of tears ran down my face, and I quickly wiped my face with the back of my hand. I crouched down trying to control my breathing as I placed my duffle bag on the ground. My mind was racing. I inhaled and exhaled one more time. After that, I stood up picking my bag back up and began to walk. I could have called a cab or sent for an Uber, but I needed to clear mind, and a nice walk would do me good. I put one foot in front of the other and zoned out.

More than ever, I wanted my mother, and I knew that one wish wouldn't come true. I had to start looking forward to the future that my mother wanted me to have. I felt that me mourning her is what had me in the position I was in right now. I knew the situation I was in now wasn't my fault, but it was time for me to live. Although my mother had an addiction, one thing that she had done was live her life the way she wanted without caring what others said about her. Her main concern was making sure that I was fed and got the education that I deserved. She made sure I was her first priority, and everything else came after that.

The more I thought about it, the more I knew that my mother would not want me to be crying and sad over her not being here for me. She would want me to live as she did, without worrying about what the next person said or did, but to live my life as I wanted to. I thought about her telling me on several occasions as I was growing up.

"Reign, all I want you to do is get an education and have a better life than I am able to give you. Fuck what other people have to say about you. So what people call you a nerd, you are one. Always remember the same ones that's talking about you right now will still be right here on the west side of Chicago when you leave here. One more thing, you have to do what's going to make you happy. Look at me. People call me out my name all the time, but do you

see me crying about it? No, you don't, because I know what I do people may see it as being wrong, but there are only two things in this world makes me happy. You're the first thing, and crack might as well be your sister because I love her second. Do what makes you feel good about being you, Reign."

I smiled thinking about how Queenie would just give it to me like it is. I continued to walk down the road in deep thought as cars passed by me.

BRENTON

My mother was going to kill me. I was so late. Not wanting to be around my father was most of the reason I was this late in the first place. My father was a dick, so every time my mother summoned me to a family dinner, I had to talk myself into going. When my mother called me today, she was raving about my brother Blake's new girlfriend. She felt I just had to come eat dinner with the family to show that I supported my brother. In other words, my dad was at home doing what he does best judging the girl because she doesn't come from money.

With my dad, it's all about connections and what our mates' family can do for us. He never wants us to marry for love. If he had it his way, we would marry his friends' daughters, sisters, or nieces. He wanted to keep the money in families that already had money, and if they weren't rich, they had to be an asset to the family. He believed that the lower class women were only good for a quick lay. I, on the other hand, objected to that. It didn't matter if the woman had money or not. As long a she was attractive, I would give her the best night of her life. If she's lucky, she can have me for a week maybe a month, but after that, I was on to the next one.

Plus, I had the pleasure of showing most of his friends' daughters the time of their lives already. Hell, I've slept with most of their wives too. It wasn't a woman at his country club that hasn't had a night or two with me. My motto was stick and move, and that's exactly what I did. Once I stuck all the women at the country club, I had to move around. My dad's choice of women for Blake and myself were girls that has been spoiled rotten by their parents. Those were the type of women that thought because they had a temper tantrum, the world would stop and bow down to them. They were shells of what a woman should be. They were evil and downright rude for no reason at all.

I know people may look at me like I'm a womanizer, but the truth is I can only do to women what they allow me to do. I don't sell them dreams of forever with a fairytale wedding, three kids, a dog, and the white picket fence. When I approach women, I let them know exactly what I'm giving, and if they choose to take it, all I offer is a night they won't forget.

Getting a woman to come home with me has never been an issue. That was until I met Reign, I went to the bar every day after I first saw her, and she turned down my advances each time. For some reason, it was like I had to have her. Maybe it was the way her hips swayed when she walked. It could be the scent of her perfume that smelled like lavender with a hint of vanilla, or the slight bow of her legs that I could picture her wrapping them around my neck as I tasted her juices.

I was in such a trance as I thought about her that I swore I just drove right past her walking on the side of the road. I shook my head slowing down looking in my rearview mirror. I would know that walk from anywhere. What the hell was she doing this far from her school, and why would she be walking on this road by herself this late?

"Damn!"

I knew once I missed this dinner I would never hear the end of it from my mother, but I couldn't just leave her on the side of the road. I mean I'm a jerk most of the time, but I wasn't heartless. I pressed the brakes on my Tesla X causing it to come to a complete stop before putting the SUV in reverse. I pulled up to the side of Reign, letting my window down.

"I don't need a ride. I'm fine, please leave me alone," Reign said walking with her head down before I could say anything to her.

"But…" was all I could get out. She never looked up but picked up her pace to get away from my car. I looked back and continued to reverse trying to talk to her she went into a light jog.

"Reign" I yelled out as a horn began blaring out and my car automatically came to a halt. Reign picked up speed she went from a jog into a run. I jumped out of my car taking off running behind her. I caught up her to and wrapped both my arms around her waist.

"Reign, I'm not trying to hurt you." She had zoned out and began to kick and scratch at my hands screaming at the top of her lungs.

"Please don't hurt me HELP! SOMEONE HELP ME!"

She twisted in my arms and began to lift her feet from the ground kicking out trying her best to get away from me. She finally dropped down making me lean over her. I held on to her tight so she wouldn't fall and hurt herself.

"Reign, please let me help you. It's me Brenton Dennis' friend from the bar. I promise I won't hurt you. I just want to help you. Calm down, baby. It's okay," I whispered close to her ear.

Reign dropped all the way down to the ground, and I sat down with her pulling her close to me as she sobbed. I rubbed my fingers through her hair massaging her scalp trying to get her to calm down.

"Is everything alright?" A car had pulled up on the side of us.

"Yes!" I answered the woman. She had a concerned look on her face.

"Ma'am, are you okay, do you need me to call someone for you?" the woman asked Reign. The muscle in my jaw twitched as I was quickly getting irritated with her.

"Reign, baby, answer her."

Reign gave a slight nod of her head. The woman didn't look too satisfied with her answer. I stood up, and Reign wrapped her arms around herself like she had to replace the comfort that I had just taken away from her. I bent down scooping her up in my arms she laid her head against my shoulder.

"Ma'am, if you would like to help us, can you open my car door for me so I can get her home?"

The woman looked at Reign sympathetically nodding her head before driving the short distance to my car opening the door. I thanked her after putting Reign in the car placing the seat belt on her. I'm not exactly sure what had happened to her before I showed up, but I knew I wouldn't like it when I found out.

I walked around to the driver side getting in the car. I slowly reached over to her stopping right before I touched her just to make sure it was ok. I wiped the tears from her face, I lightly touched the left side of her face, and she flinched. I turned the light on in the car, and the left side of her face was swollen. Her lip was bust on that side too. Anger flooded me, and I wanted to hurt whoever had hurt her. I pulled out my phone and called Dennis, but there was no answer. I called the number to the bar, and there was no answer there either.

I put on my seatbelt and pulled off. I didn't know where she stayed, I could take her to my parents' house, but I didn't want to hear my father's mouth. I made a U-turn and began to make the trip back towards Harvard. Once I made it close to campus, I looked over at Reign to ask her for her address, but she was sleeping so peacefully that I didn't want to wake her up. I could tell she had a long day. I made a judgment call and took her to my house. Once I parked in the garage, I got out the car went over to her picking her up. She wrapped her arms around my neck instantly without waking up.

"Mom, why did you leave me?" Her voice was soft I looked down at her she was talking in her sleep.

I took her to my room carefully placing her in the bed. I began to take off her shoes and socks I lifted her pulling off her jacket when I got to her jeans I unzipped them and was just about to pull them down. She woke up swinging her arms wildly, kicking her feet outward, and let out a piercing scream. I moved away from her throwing my hands in the air.

"Reign, it's me, Brenton. I will not hurt you, calm down."

She turned her head looking at me with her eyes wide. She sat up and broke down crying rocking and hugging herself, so I walked over to the bed slowly sitting down beside her. I wrapped my arms around her and just held her until she stopped crying.

"Where am I?" She asked after she completely calmed down.

"You're at my house." I gave her my address.

"If you want, I can take you home, or you can send the address to one of your friends. I promise I won't hurt you either way."

"I know," she replied while looking me straight in my eyes.

"How do you know that?" I asked her curiously.

"The way you came off at my job, if something did happen, you would be the first person they look for," she stated without blinking her eyes.

"Actually the first person they would look for would be the last person you were with." She gave a slight nod if I had of blinked I would've missed it.

"Do you want to talk about why you were walking on the side of the road?" She shook her head while replying.

"No."

"Have you eaten anything?" I asked her.

"Not since lunch," she quietly replied then began to stare off in the distant.

"How about I order take out, and you can go take a bath to try and relax. By the time you're done, the food should be here." She nodded her head again, so I walked in the master bathroom and started her bath.

I really didn't have anything in my house for a woman to bath in, so I put my body wash in the water to make her bubbles. I walked back into the room pulling out one of my t-shirts and a pair of my basketball shorts. I knew my shorts would probably fall off of her, but I wanted her to feel comfortable and safe.

"Your bath is ready. I won't come back in the room until you let me know you're ready for me to."

I walked out of my room and closed the door. I went to the living room and called for a pizza. I wasn't sure what she liked on her pizza, so I ordered half with the works and the other half cheese.

I sat on the couch just thinking and everything in me is telling me that someone had hurt her besides the obvious bruises on her face and busted lip. For some reason I just wanted to make everything better for her, I wanted to protect her. I wanted to hurt the person that hurt her. My doorbell rang out through the house, so I grabbed my wallet pulling out a hundred dollar bill. I opened the door handed it to the pizza man got our food and closed the door without telling him to keep the change. I guess he got the idea with the closed door. I sat the pizza on the counter and Reign started screaming my name. I ran to the bathroom busting through the door looking around as if someone was in there with her. She looked at me.

"I didn't mean to startle you, but I've been calling you for about five minutes." She looked at me then covered herself with her with her arms.

"What's wrong?"

"I need a dry towel, and I didn't want to just go through your things." She made sure to keep herself covered as I turned going to the towel warmer handing her a towel.

She reached one hand out of the tub, and that's when I saw bruises all over her arms and stomach. I sat down in a chair that I keep in the corner of the bathroom.

"We need to talk about this." Her lip quivered, and she nodded her head.

REIGN

I sat in the tub that was big enough for three adults to get in dropping the towel that Brenton had just given me over the top half of my body. He sat in the chair staring in my eyes as if he could see through me. I looked down at the towel that was now soaked from the water, and then my eyes met his again. A foreign feeling came over me, something I hadn't felt in a long time— I felt safe. I couldn't understand why out of all the people I had come in contact with over these last few years it was him that gave me the feeling of safety.

The first day I saw him in the bar, he was coming at me like a blood-thirsty hound, but today, he was showing another side of him. I had dated Blake for months and didn't feel the comfort that I feel now while sitting in this man's bathroom naked in front of him. As hard as he tried to get me in his bed last week, I would've thought I would see nothing but lust in his eyes. At this moment, lust wasn't there. It was concern that someone had hurt me. I leaned back in the tub, and I pulled my lower lip in, biting down on it to stop it from quivering.

"On this day three years ago, I lost my mother." My voice was barely above a whisper. I stopped taking a deep breath to stop the tears that I felt from running down my face. I cleared my throat before continuing.

"I lost her two weeks before my eighteenth birthday, and the same day I found out I had gotten into Harvard. My mother wasn't a perfect woman. She was a drug addict. Most people would think that made her a horrible person and mother, but she wasn't. I looked at it as everyone had problems. Some people are alcoholics, workaholics, sex addicts; you name it. Most of those people will beat on their spouse and kids, rape them, or some other form of emotional abuse, but not my mother. She was a smart woman, and she taught me a lot of things in those seventeen years. She just had a habit.

My mother kept a roof over my head. It may not have been like this, but it was somewhere to stay dry and warm. I may have had to survive off of peanut butter and jelly at times, but I was well fed. My clothes and shoes may not have been the best, but I had those and no matter how high my mother was or how late she stayed out at night, she made sure to be at home every morning to walk me to the bus stop before school."

Tears were running down my face, and Brenton was now sitting behind me with his feet in my bath water running his fingers through my hair and scalp.

"The day my mother died, our routine hadn't changed except the fact that I knew something was wrong with her. She looked sick. I had complained about the mattress that I slept on. That day I wished I had a mother that was better than the one I had. I wanted a mother that would have been able to buy me the things that I needed and wanted, only to have to leave school that day to find out my mother was dying. From all the drugs she was using, she had a bad heart. I got in the bed with her for the time and laid with until she left me."

I laid my head back on his leg and lightly wiped the tears from my face.

"So how did you end up walking on the side of the road today?" he asked me with concern in his voice.

"I was trying to forget," I told him softly

"The only male friend I have asked me to come with him for the weekend. He wanted to help me make new memories, happier ones so that I wouldn't wake up in the middle of the night crying out for my mother. So I wouldn't want to stay in my house every year on this day and just cry. The only thing is that he made this day way worst for me, I hate this day. I just feel like everything that happens to me that's bad happens on this day."

By this time, I was sobbing, and Brenton had picked me up and wrapped me in a warm towel. He carried me to his bed carefully laying me down on it as if I was an infant. He covered me in a light blanket and let me continue to cry. Once my tears subsided, he looked down at me.

"Tell me his name," Brenton demanded. I shook my head no to him. "Did he get a chance to..." He stopped not letting the word come out.

"No," I answered softly he let out a breath.

"But he beat you; you're bruised almost everywhere." I shook my head at him.

"Don't shake your head no at me. I know that whoever he is was rough your cocoa skin is turning black and blue, your face is swollen, and your lip is split. Just tell me who it is so that I can have him arrested." Brenton was now pacing the floor his eyes were filled with rage.

"He's rich, so he would just pay the judge off, and his parents would probably buy the entire justice system." Brenton stopped pacing looking at me as if I had lost my mind.

"So what he's rich. I'm rich too, and I'm pretty sure he doesn't have as much money as my family does. We can own the system. All you have to do is tell me who he is."

I looked around Brenton's room. Yes, I could he had money, but his house was nothing compared to the mansion I just left.

"Brenton, I really appreciate everything that you have done for me, but this is just something I don't want to do. I've been through enough, and I don't want to have to be outcast and lose everything that I have worked so hard for. I don't want to lose my scholarship because of a couple of bruises that will heal with time. I can't afford to pay for school out of my pocket, and the only thing that my mother requested of me before dying was for me to get an education and become someone that she could be proud of. I won't let her down."

Brenton looked down at me like he understood where I was coming from.

"I understand what you are saying you want to beat the odds, you are your mother's legacy, and you want to keep your promise to her." He grabbed my hand, and his eyes met mine. "But, in making her proud, you have to be able to live with yourself and the demons that come along with you personally. Can you say that keeping this to yourself and not putting this person behind bars will make you proud of you? Can you live with this secret you want to hold so tight?" He kissed the palm of my hand. "Are you ready to eat?" he asked, changing the subject.

I nodded my head, yes, and he left the room.

I looked down at the palm of my hand that he had kissed and a warm sensation went through me thinking of the moment his warm, soft lips touched there. A surge of heat went through me that I had never felt before heating me to the core. My inner thighs had become wet with my juices, and my womanly parts came alive and began to pulsate at the thought of those same lips kissing other places on my body.

How could one man kiss me there some many times and my body never react to him, but Brenton kissed me just after being around him not even twenty-four hours and my entire body is on fire? I got up and put on the clothes that he had laid out for me. The shorts sat at the top of my butt, and every time I moved, they would inch down off of me.

I cleaned up the mess that was made and pulled the blankets back over the bed right as Brenton came back in with a huge plate of pizza and two sodas. He set the pizza on the bed between us and soda on the nightstand.

"I wasn't sure what you toppings you eat, so I got everything." I looked at him and smiled as my stomach growled loudly. He laughed a little and nodded his head towards the pizza, and I dug in.

I took in his perfectly tanned skin, medium build, black hair, and kaleidoscope eyes, and I took a deep breath. Although I had seen him for a week straight I really never paid much attention to him until now. His cleanly shaved face gave him the look of a teenager, but everything else about him spoke volumes of masculinity. He looked up at me staring at him and smiled my mouth went dry and other parts of me got wet as I stared back at him. He had the perfect smile too. I went back to eating my food. Once we finished, Brenton turned on a chick flick, and we watched TV until I went to sleep.

* * *

I WOKE up sweating looking around the room. I sat up in the bed and Brenton ran from the corner from a chair he was sitting in. I blew out a sigh of relief once he was at my side.

"It's ok. You're safe." I nodded my head lying back down and fell right back to sleep.

* * *

I WOKE up to the sun shining brightly through the bedroom windows. Brenton was back in the chair in the corner sleeping peacefully.

"You want something to eat?" he asked me without opening his eyes.

"No, but can you take me home?" Brenton got up out of his chair opened the drawer to the nightstand handing me a toothbrush.

"I will take you wherever you want to go, but whatever you do today, please don't try and go into work with your face like that."

I got up going into the bathroom looking at my face for the first time. I was so caught up in my emotions yesterday that I hadn't thought to look at my face. Blake had smacked me so hard yesterday that I saw spots for a minute. I thought about the events that happened and thinking about how hard his hand had landed across my face. The entire left side of my face was swollen, including my eye, my face was bruised.

"Oh my god!" I stood in the mirror staring at myself. How was I going to explain this to Amber? She was going to go insane, and I'm pretty sure I would have to bail her out of jail after she sees my face. Brenton stepped into the bathroom and watched me stare in the mirror.

"My roommate is going to have a fit and probably need a good lawyer when she's done," I told him without looking at him.

"You wouldn't have to get her lawyer if you just tell me who did this to you." He stared me down. I diverted my eyes from him trying to look everywhere except him.

"No!" I raised my voice, walking past him out of the bathroom.

"If you're so worried about your roommate, you can always stay here until your face is completely healed." He walked over to the bed sitting down.

"No, I can't impose on you like that. Plus, this week is finals, so I can't miss school, and I have to go to work." I watched Brenton contemplate what I was telling him.

"I could call your professors and tell them that you had a family emergency. They will let you take your finals online, and I will give you the week off at work," he said it like it was just that simple, and I wasn't sure how he could give me a week off work. I know that he and Dennis were good friends, but how was he capable of giving me a week off? He moved at my questioning gaze.

"I have ways of getting what I want, and I can make all of this happen." I nodded my head.

"No, I'm good. You can drop me off at home, and I'll just deal with everything on my own."

I walked over to the chair that my bag was sitting in the corner and began pulling out clothes to wear home. Shortly after, we were sitting in front of my apartment building. Brenton grabbed my hand.

"Are you sure you don't want to spend the week at my house? I can make sure you have everything you need." I gave him a weak smile.

"I will be okay I promise. Plus, I have to go to work. I still have bills that need to be paid. I can't put my life at a standstill because of a couple of bruises."

Brenton looked at me like he was contemplating something, he opened his mouth to say something then stopped. His multicolored eyes gazed into mine.

"I have an event coming up in a couple of weeks, and I would like it if you would come with me?" I shook my head before the words came out of my mouth.

"I don't think that would be a good idea." He seemed a little defeated.

"What if I paid you? It would help you out while helping myself as well. I can give you thirty thousand dollars."

My mouth dropped open. That money could help me out a lot, but at what cost? I closed my eyes. This man keeps surprising me. Once I was over the shock of the large amount of money that he offered me, I dropped my hand from his. He looked at me then grabbed my hand again.

"Money is how I ended up in this predicament I'm in now." I pointed my finger to my face.

"I won't accept any handouts. I once thought a friend was helping me and soon found out that he felt since he was giving me money here and there that he was entitled to all of me. I refuse to go through that again, and I refuse to have to fight just because people thank if they help you they own you."

I felt the tears coming. I was choking on sadness and anger all at one time. Brenton pulled my hand up to his mouth and kissed the palm of it. All of a sudden, my feelings began to settle. The softness of his lips and his intense gaze was like a jolt to my hormones. This man made me feel things I couldn't explain just by doing the simplest things.

"I'm not him. I would never put my hands on you, and I would never take what you're not giving. I'm not accepting no from you right now. Just think about it and let me know if you have a change of heart in a week."

To him, it was settled he thought. I would have a change of heart, but I knew I wasn't changing my mind.

"Okay," was my only response before opening the car door. Brenton hurried out of the car coming to the passenger side. He helped me out of the car and grabbed my duffle bag from the back seat. He walked me to the door.

"I have it from here." He handed me my bag and turned to walk away.

"Thank you for everything I really appreciate your help." Brenton took a couple of steps back, placing his hand on my cheek. He went into his pocket pulled out a card handing it to me.

"Call me if you need anything I don't care what it is or the time of day." I nodded my head at him without looking up in his face.

"Take care of yourself, Reign," he whispered in my ear turning around going back to the car. I opened the door walking up the stairs to my apartment.

I went to the window, and Brenton was still sitting in front of the building. I pulled the shade up and waved at him, and only then did he pull off. I took a deep breath and exhaled while sitting on the sofa. I truly was exhausted. I leaned my head back and drifted off to sleep.

* * *

"What the hell happened to your face?" I jumped up staring into Ambers angry eyes, and all I could think was there goes the neighborhood. Amber looked at me waiting for me to answer her question. I really should've thought of a lie to tell her before I fell asleep. She waited impatiently for an answer that I really didn't want to give. The minutes that passed by with her brow beating me felt like hours. She wanted an explanation, and she wanted it now, but I was too exhausted to come up with a lie that would appease her, so I stayed silent.

"Did Blake cut your tongue out after he put his hands on you?" she asked her New York accent was in full effect now. I blinked my eyes at her.

"No!" I responded quickly. "It's not what you think, Amber." I stood up trying to walk away from her.

She reached out grabbing my wrist, and I winched as she looked down at my wrist and went into a lot of expletives.

"What I think, no matter of fact what I know is that I'm going to hurt him."

Amber went walked to her room and came back with an arm full of stuff. Within seconds, Amber was pulling off her clothes and changing right in front of me. The next thing to go was her medium sized hoop earrings. She put a large amount of Vaseline on her face, balled her hair up into a ponytail, and wrapped a scarf around her head. She finished off her look with a pair of brass knuckles that look like they were custom made for her small hands, she put a can of mace in her pocket with something that looked like a key ring, but I'm pretty sure it was a small knife.

Amber was standing in front of me with. A pair of black loose fitting jogging pants a black sports bra, and black steel toes. You can take the girl out of Brooklyn, but you can't take Brooklyn out of the girl. at that moment I knew I should've stayed at Brenton's house, Amber was really about to go to jail. Although the situation was bad, I couldn't have loved my friend any more than I did at this moment.

Amber really never had friends growing up. She said that most of the girls that she grew up with hated her because of her light complexion and beautiful face, which is sad because she's a great friend. For that reason, she hung out with boys. With me being the only true female friend she's ever had, she's very protective. She was out for blood, and I had to get this under control so she wouldn't get kicked out of school.

"Amber, calm down he's not worth it I assure you I'm fine. I may have a couple of bruises, but I'm okay," I told her earnestly.

"Did he..." She evaluated me cautiously not finishing her statement.

"No, he didn't get a chance to do anything besides what you see now." She still side eyed me.

"The fact that he tried is why I feel he's worth it." Amber walked over to me and sat on the couch, and she pulled my hand into hers. "If I would've thought for one second that he would do something like this, I would've never encouraged you becoming friends with him. I feel so bad right now and to think that I let him in the house and left you here alone. I'm so sorry." She gave my hand a squeeze.

"It's not your fault, neither one of us thought he would've been the prick he turned out to be. I know where he gets it from though. His dad is a complete asshole." I rolled my eyes dramatically.

Amber sat staring at me waiting for me to give her the gory details of my day of hell, but I didn't feel like talking about it. I didn't want to revisit that day, so I stood up feeling Amber's inquisitive stare.

"I'm going to bed." She quickly stood up.

"You're not going to tell me what happened to you?" She stood with her hands on her tiny waist and mouth gaped open with a questioning expression on her face.

"What I will tell you is he has a sweet mother, and I feel like she's suffering enough having to deal with the two men in her life. The last thing I would want to do is cause her any more trouble, so what I want to do and want you to do is forget this day ever happened, okay."

I walked into my room before she could respond and closed my door. I know what I did was a bit much, especially since I know Amber would go to war for me. I just wanted to forget that day ever happened. I pulled off the clothes that I had on for the day when a card fell to the floor. I picked it up and smiled thinking about the well-toned tall, handsome man with the multicolored eyes. I rubbed my fingers across the bold black letters on the card. "Brenton P Thomas," I said aloud to myself and smiled before placing the card in my wallet and going to shower.

* * *

I WAS sleep having the same dream that I had for the last four years, and I felt the tears running down my face. I heard myself crying out for my mother as usual, but there was something different about it. I felt a weight holding me down, then a deep voice whispered in my ear.

"It's okay, Reign. I'm right here. Wake up, baby."

Before I opened my eyes, there were soft kisses placed on both of my eyes then down both cheeks. Then a kiss placed on my mouth that was so sensual. I opened my eyes blinking rapidly to clear my vision, and I was looking deeply into the beautiful, but concerned eyes of Brenton. I said his name softly aloud, and he pulled both of my hands up to his mouth kissing the palms of them. I looked around my room trying to clear my head.

"How did you get in here?" He smiled at me.

"Should I leave?" he asked, pushing up from the bed.

"No." I pulled him down back to me urgently.

"Please don't," I continued to say before placing my lips over his feverishly.

I put my tongue in his mouth flicking and twirling it around his. Brenton intensified the kiss and began doing things I didn't know was humanly possible to be done. I heard a low moan the air and realized it was my own voice that I heard. I gently bit down on his bottom lip he groaned pulling away from me. He took a deep breath then began to put feather kisses along my jawline and neck.

It was as if this man had the road map to my clitoris as it began to throb, and I felt my vaginal walls contracting. I began to bring my thighs together trying to cause a small amount of friction to the area that pulsated with need. He lightly caressed my legs up to my torso as my stomach muscles clenched under his touch I exhaled deeply.

"Sit up," Brenton commanded. I hurried sitting up and holding my arms up in the air as he slowly pulled my tank top over my head. He lightly pushed me back down to the bed and kissing and licking his way to my breasts.

"You are so beautiful. I will sit at your feet and serve you anything you want for the rest of my life."

He held eye contact with me, and I noticed his multicolored eyes getting darker with longing. My breathing increased as I craved his touch, missing his mouth on me. I sat up a little pulling him down to me and attacked his mouth with mines. Just hearing the words, he said created a bigger ache between my legs. Brenton moved down to my breasts flicking his tongue over one before putting my nipple in his mouth and sucking hard. Brenton was slowly and lightly caressing my body with one hand while having his mouth somewhere else was causing a whirlwind of passion and need to my mind and body. He was completely on top of me and moving my legs open with his knees never taking his mouth away from my nipple while holding most of his weight up on his elbows.

He moved from one breast to the other then took his right hand and began to fondle the nipple that he had just left. I arched my back under him inhaled and exhaled in small breaths as my body began to tingle all over. I pulled at his short spiked hair not sure if I wanted him to stop the treacherous things he was doing to my body or continue. My body was on fire and knowing what it wanted, my body began to move all on its own. My hips began to rotate at its own pace to its own rhythm. Brenton began trailing his hand down my side going to the center of the ache. He adjusted himself on me so that I could feel the hardness within his pants

I moved a little using my hand going into his jogging pants getting right to the matter at hand. I grasped the thickness of his wood, and he exhaled a breath causing cool air to hit where his mouth had been. I lightly caressed his shaft as he put his mouth back on my nipple, and I began to stroke him up and down. Listening to the moans that came from him as I did my best to please him, Brenton used his finger to collect some of my wetness before he began to play with my pleasure bud. The intensity of his mouth on my breasts and his fingers at work below on me sent a different surge through my body. My hips began to move a little faster, and my hand pumped him like my life depended on it. He bit down on my nipple tugging it just a little, both of our bodies stiffened at the same time. I yelled his name at the top of my lungs as he said mine in more of a grunt. He moved his finger a couple more times, and I felt my juices leave my body just as he came out in my hand.

I woke up spasming, breathing hard, and sweating with one of my hands in my shorts. I sat up looking around the room for Brenton, and of course, he was nowhere in sight because it was a wet dream. I stood up, getting a towel. I needed a cold shower and fast. I turned on the lights in the room and couldn't believe my eyes. I guess I needed to change my sheets first.

I walked out of my room the next morning still in a daze from the dream I had the previous night. Amber came out of the kitchen with a smirk on her face.

*　*　*

"Good morning, Amber!" I mumbled and continued to head to the bathroom.

"Good morning, Reign." She gazed at me with a smirk on her face, and her smile became wider as she watched me make my way towards the bathroom.

"Who is Brenton and is he still in the room?" She laughed hard before running towards her room.

I picked up my pace to try to catch her. She turned sideways using her socked feet to slide into her room the door closed, and I heard the lock click right afterwards. I shook my head I can't believe that I was that loud having a damn dream. I went to handle my hygiene then went to talk to Amber. I didn't want to talk about what had happened over the weekend, but I would make sure to fill her in about Brenton and how he helped me.

*　*　*

"What the hell do you mean my balance is five cents?" I sat and listened attentively as the customer service representative went over my balance and last five transactions. Trying to figure out what was going on.

"I never wrote a check to the United Negro College Fund. I'm a student at Harvard. Why would I do that?" I stated, getting more frustrated as the representative continued to explain what the exact transaction that was about to have me a homeless college drop out.

"Yes ma'am, I would like for it to be investigated. I'm telling you I didn't do it. I don't even own checks, so how could I write one?"

My hands started shaking, and everything around me began to start moving as I tried to figure out what the hell was going on. I had three thousand eight hundred thirty-five dollars and seven cents in my account last week. I tried to swipe my card for six dollars today, and my card was declined. I checked my account on my app and when I saw five cents in there, I thought they were having some kind of glitch in the system, so I called only to find out that what I saw was the real amount left in my account. I laid my head down on the table in the break room feeling the beginning of a migraine starting. I answered the necessary questions that fraud prevention asked me before hopelessly ending the call.

I had no idea what I was going to do. All I knew is that my life had gone from bad to worse in a matter of weeks. On top of all that, Blake had been more than a pain in my ass in every class we had together. He had even started coming back to the Bar and Grill trying to give me a hard time there, but Dennis stopped that before it even started. I was grateful for that, but there was nothing that Dennis could do about how he treated me during seminars or on campus. For the most part, I tried to stay far away from him.

I sat completely straight up in my chair, I closed my eyes and rubbed at my temples willing the massive headache to go away. I felt tears running down my face from the pounding in my head and from the realization that Blake was behind my account being empty.

I thought about one of his hockey teammates that he introduced me to, I think his name was Christian, and he bragged about his family owning the franchise of banks that I have my account at. I cursed myself knowing that I was utterly screwed. There would be nothing that could be done about my account being hacked. I was so zoned out that I didn't know Dennis had come in the room and sat down across from me.

"Are you ok, Reign?" Dennis asked his voice was etched with concern. I have no idea how many times he asked me if I was okay. When I opened my eyes, Dennis was sitting in front of me his face was an expression of worry. I wiped the tears from my face and cleared my throat.

REIGN

"I'm fine," my voice cracked as the words came from my mouth. I cleared my voice one more time and tried again. "I'm okay," I answered that sounded a little better.

Before Dennis could ask me anything else, I got up going into the employee's bathroom locking the door behind me. I heard Dennis chair slide across the floor letting me know that he had left the break room. My head began to swarm, so I grasped the sink holding on, trying not to fall. I turned the cold water on knowing I had to get myself together so that I could start my shift. I washed my face with the cold water several times before I felt a little better. There was a light knock on the door.

"Reign, are you okay in there?" Amber asked from the other side of the door. I should've known that Dennis would send her back here to see what was going on with me. I didn't respond to her. I took a deep breath.

"Dennis told me he found you back here crying. Whatever is going on, we can fix it together no matter what it is or who we have to kill," Amber stated matter of factly. I chuckled a little. "Open the door, Reign. We are going to be okay."

I heard someone else whisper something then Amber say something that was muffled back.

"What the hell?" I heard Amber saying clearly.

I had no idea what was going on, on the other side of this door, but I had a feeling it was only about to make my life worse then what it was already. I started seeing spots in front of my eyes. I closed my eyes opening the door up and then opened them back up. Amber and Dennis were standing together, and Amber had my phone in her hand looking at the screen with her mouth open. I walked over to them.

"Why the horrible expressions, you guys found my nudes?" I joked with them trying to see what they were looking at that had them looking terrified. Amber moved away from holding my phone to her chest. My head started pounding harder than it had ever before.

"May I have my phone, please?" She shook her head no and kept the look of terror on her face.

I took a big step standing right in front of her causing her to back up into Dennis. I pulled at her hand that she had my phone in. I glanced down at the screen through blurred spotted vision. I stared at the phone until I got a clear view of a naked dead me sitting on the floor eyes and mouth open with my wrist split and bleeding. The caption in big bold red letters **KILL YOURSELF**. The door to break room opened, Amber and Dennis stood in front of me with their mouths moving, but no words were coming out. My vision swirled Amber and Dennis into one, and I blacked out.

BRENTON

Brenton I was sitting in my office on the phone with my grandfather going over some of the things that he's expecting of me for the up and coming gala. I absolutely loved the old man. He's been here for me more than my father has. I listened to him go over the event then he told me that instead of my parents and brother staying in a hotel like they usually do every year, they were staying at the house. As he told me that, I went on the internet to book the penthouse suite at the Ritz Carlton in San Antonio, Texas. There was no way I was staying at the mansion with my father, especially since I wanted to bring Reign with me. Although, my grandfather's family estate was almost eleven thousand square feet and sat on one hundred acres of land with three guest houses and a horse ranch, that still wasn't enough space to get away from my father's ego. As I started to make the reservation, I had gotten tagged in something on my Facebook page. I clicked the notification and what I stared at caused my heart rate to increase.

"Are you there, Brenton?" I couldn't believe what I was seeing on my computer screen. What the hell was wrong with people these days?

"Benny, are you there?" I cleared my throat before speaking.

"Yes grandfather, I'm here, but can I call you back? I have an emergency." As soon as the word yes left his mouth, I hung up grabbed my car keys and sprinted out of the office. I called Dennis phone.

"Hey, Dennis is Reign on the schedule for today?" I asked before he was able to say hello.

"Yes, but I hope you're not coming to harass the poor girl because she's already having a bad day." I swallowed hard. If she hadn't yet seen the image that I had seen a few minutes earlier, then her bad day was about to get way worse.

"Dennis, go on your Facebook page there is something that you and about five thousand other people were tagged in about five minutes ago." I waited for him to look at the image.

"What the hell?" was what left his mouth.

"Shit! I have to call you back." He hung up the phone.

I laid into my horn as a driver cut me off. I swerved around them and accelerated my car again, and I broke almost every traffic law there was to get to the bar. I came to a halt taking the handicapped parking space in front of the bar. I got out of my car, and I could see the smoke coming off my tires. I ran into the bar looking around. Dennis or Reign wasn't on the floor, so I hastily walked to the back of the bar in the direction of the break room. One of the waitresses blocked me off.

"I'm sorry sir, you can't go back there." She held her hands up in front of me.

"Move, or I will have your ass fired." She stood in front of me with her hands on her hips. I tried to go around her, and she pushed me backwards.

"You can't go back there!" she yelled.

"I heard you the first time you said it and as you can see I'm still going to proceed, so please move out of my way, or I will move you." She crossed her arms over her chest, and I politely picked her up moving her out of my way.

"I'm calling the police!" she yelled thinking that would stop me. I turned to take a look at her.

"Good, and when they get here, they can escort you out because you're fired," I stated before walking into the break room in time to catch Reign as she dropped down to the floor.

"Get me a cold towel," I told the girl that was standing in front of Dennis with a concerned look on her face.

I sat on the floor holding Reign close to me. The girl stood there like she was in shock. I snapped my fingers getting her attention. She blinked a couple of times before nodding her head and running into the bathroom. She came back over to me with a white wet hand towel. She folded it then laying it across Reign's forehead. I took the other end of the towel and blotted her face. I shifted her weight to one side pulling my phone out of my pocket and handing it to Dennis.

"Call Dr. Wong for me and tell him to meet us at my house."

Dennis did as I asked while the girl that went and got the towel sat on the floor on the side of Reign and began to rub her head and whisper in her ear.

"Excuse me?" the girl asked me with her face frowned at me.

"I'm sorry. What are you talking about?" She raised her eyebrow at me.

"Thank you for stopping my friend from hitting the floor, but she's not going anywhere with you," she stated matter of factly.

I looked at the light-skinned girl with the New York accent and figured that she was Amber the roommate. I didn't know if Reign had told her about me, but I didn't have time to argue with her about what needed to be done for Reign.

"Hi Amber, I'm Brenton, an acquaintance of Reign. I know that you may not know who I am, but we have to get your friend looked at. With everything that's going on, I would prefer we take her back to my house for that. I don't have time to go back and forth, but you're more than welcome to come with us, or Dennis can bring you by the house."

I didn't wait for her to respond as I picked Reign up. Dennis opened the door, and before I could walk out, the police were coming up the hall. I guess the waitress wasn't playing about calling the cops.

"Mr. Thomas, we got a call about someone trespassing," Officer Walker stated, looking at Reign in my arms.

"I'm sorry that you guys had to come all this way for a misunderstanding, but you guys didn't come in vain." I looked past them to the waitress that had threatened to call them. I took a good look at her nametag.

"Brandy, you're fired. Can you gentlemen escort her off the property, and when you're done, I need an escort to my house," I told them walking pass her.

"Who is he supposed to be?" I heard Brandy say as I passed her.

"He's part owner of the bar. Sorry Brandy, leave your badge at the bar," I heard Dennis reply to her, and if I'm not mistaken, Amber was laughing following right behind me.

As I hurried to my car, Amber opened the door to the back seat for me, and I gently laid Reign in the back. Amber got in the front seat and closed the door.

"Dennis said he'd be about thirty minutes behind us," she stated. I nodded my head and pulled out of the parking lot just in time for the officers to get in their car and turn on the sirens.

I followed between them making the twenty-minute drive to my house in half the time. The doctor was standing outside the door waiting for me. I handed Amber the key to open the door instead of going to the garage. She opened the front door in a hast helping the old doctor with his bag and then cleared the couch for me to lie Reign down.

As he started the exam, Amber and I sat at the island in the kitchen watching the doctor.

"I have to do something with my hands," Amber voiced as she walked away from me going to the refrigerator pulling out potatoes, steak, vegetables, and whatever else that I had in there.

Since Reign was here the last time and I had nothing edible in the house, I made sure I ordered groceries to be delivered that night that she left.

"Where are the pots and pans?" Amber asked. I pointed to the cabinets they were behind.

"Brenton?" I looked over at Amber.

"Yes," I replied waiting for her to get what she wanted off her chest.

"Reign told me that you helped her out a couple of weeks ago." I sat at the island looking between Amber and Dr. Wong waiting for her to continue.

"Reign is my best friend, she's my only friend, she's had a rough start, and after what she through with that asshole recently..." Amber stopped again as if she was in deep thought. "Anyway, if you don't have her best interest at heart, please just leave her alone now. I remember when you first came to the Bar and Grill you were disrespectful to her. We both know exactly what you wanted from her, and if that's still the case, leave her the hell alone." She stared at me.

"I can assure you that is not my intent with her." I held her gaze. She broke eye contact to add butter and green peppers to a skillet.

"I have a question." She stopped cutting vegetables and looked at me.

"Do you know who she was with a couple weeks ago when I found her on the side of the road?" She smirked at me.

"If she didn't tell you, neither will I, but I do have a feeling he has something to do with all that she has gone through today." I raised a brow at her.

"What do you mean by that?"

"Before that horrible picture went viral, someone hacked her bank account. Don't say anything to her about it. She doesn't know that I know. When Dennis came to get me early because she was crying, she left her phone open on her bank app. I have a feeling that the same guy that she was out with that weekend has something to do with that too."

Amber continued to move comfortably around my kitchen. I wanted to demand she tell me who this asshole was that was doing this to Reign, but I knew that she wouldn't betray her friend like that, so I took a different approach.

"Since you don't want to talk to me about Reign, how about we talk about something that you are trying to hide, but I see it clearly."

Amber froze like she was caught with her hand in the cookie jar.

Her expression was amusing, and I would've laughed if what I had to say wasn't a serious situation.

"What's that?" She began to cautiously move around the kitchen." I smirked at her.

"Well, you're talking to me about your friend, so I think it's only fair that I talk to you about Dennis. Before you get on the defensive end, I can tell that you like him a lot and he you." I paused taking in the feelings that she expressed on her face and seeing if she was going to object to the subject. She didn't, so I continued.

"Dennis hasn't had things so easy in life either. Only his closest of friends know exactly what he has been through and that's because we had to help him through it. He's a good guy, and I can tell you're a strong woman. I admire that about you, but if you feel like you won't be able to give him what he deserves, stop while you're ahead."

Dennis had said something about Amber before I met Reign, I knew that he really liked her, and I understand why he would. Amber was beautiful and didn't take any shit from anyone.

"I don't know about all of that," she said, looking at the floor. I cocked my head to the left trying to find her angle.

"Brenton, if I can be honest with you, there may come a time when I cannot be here for Reign, and she will need someone. Regardless of what happens between you two, if she needs a friend, I need you to be that for her. I know that this is a lot to ask of you, but from the way you continue to look at her every couple of seconds, I know you won't let me down. Dennis is a great man, but that will never happen." Amber had a faraway look in her eyes.

With what Dennis told me about her, I knew that she would be perfect for him, but after what she just relayed to me, it made me wonder what she was hiding from everyone. She may not have been good with hiding her feelings, but whatever secret she was keeping, she is holding on to it for dear life.

"Mr. Thomas, can you come here please?" Dr. Wong had called out. I turned leaving Amber to cooking to see what was going on with Reign. I walked over to them, and Reign's eyes were fluttering as she focused on me.

"Reign has had an anxiety attack, and her blood pressure was a little elevated, but due to the problems that she advised me that happened within these last couple of weeks, that should be expected. Here are some meds that will help her get through the rest of today, but here's a prescription for her she should take these as needed. I want her to relax so no work or school for the next two weeks." He handed me the piece of paper and put everything back into his bag. I handed him a check, and he prepared to walk out of the door.

"How do you like your steak?" Amber held up the steak.

"Medium rare," I answered her as the door open, and Dennis walked in the house looking between Amber and me.

I walked the doctor out and headed back over to Reign, and she looked like she was ready to pass out again. Her cocoa skin was pale, her eyes were red and puffy, and her hair was all over her head. I could see the stress lines on her forehead and her bottom lip quivered as if she was about to burst into tears at any moment. I went and sat beside her grasping her hand into mine then kissing it.

"I don't know how I'm going to fix this, Brenton." She pulled her hand from mine hugging herself rocking back and forth. If she kept this up, she would have a nervous breakdown right in front of me.

"Don't worry about it now. We can talk later. You have a couple of weeks to figure out a solution. Right now though I think you should eat something, Amber has made us steak." She got up, and I followed her into the kitchen.

We walked up on Dennis and Amber having a heated debate about something. Once they finally noticed our presence, they stopped, putting on weak smiles. Amber walked over to the table with two plates in her hand she sat them down in front of Reign and me. Dennis followed behind her with their plates sitting them on the table. I walked over to the wine cooler getting a bottle for us to have with dinner.

"So do either of you want to tell us what you were discussing during that heated exchange?" I took my seat at the table. Both Amber and Dennis narrowed their eyes at me then looked away.

"I don't think this is an appropriate time. Let's just enjoy dinner," Amber replied while cutting into her steak.

We finished the rest of our meal in silence. About an hour after eating Amber stood up stretching.

"Are you going to be okay here for the night?" she asked Reign. Reign nodded her head. I gazed over at her then got up to walk Amber and Dennis out.

"I don't know you that well, but after what Dennis and Reign told me about you, I'm trusting you to take care of my friend. She's been through a lot. I know what type of man you are, and the last thing she needs is someone that's going to toy with her feelings." I held my hand up to stop her.

"Let me finish," Amber sternly demanded. I nodded my head for her to continue.

"If you hurt her in any shape, form, or fashion I will slice your nuts off, bronze them, and give them to Reign as a parting gift."

Amber gave me a smile that didn't reach her eyes. I could tell that she was serious about her threat. Just knowing that the pint-sized person would try it gave me a feeling of being kicked below the belt, I felt my balls drawing tight to my body in a protective way.

"Regardless of what you think of me, you need to know that I care for Reign. I would never intentionally hurt her. She's so different from any of the women I usually deal with. All I want to do is help her. I guarantee you that I have her best interest at heart."

Amber stared me down waiting to see a hint of dishonesty in my eyes. She finally turned to get in the car where Dennis stood holding the car door open for her. He looked at me giving me a weak smile with a dreadful expression. Once he closed the car door, he stepped over to me.

"For both of our sakes, I hope your intentions are good because my nuts are on the line too." Dennis shook as if a chill passed through him and walked to the driver side getting into the car.

I went back into the house and Reign was lying on the couch with tears in her eyes. I couldn't imagine having the type of day that she's had. All I wanted to do was make everything right for her. I wanted the feisty girl that I had met not too long ago. Laying on my couch in the fetal position, she looked so fragile and weak. I guess after being strong for so long there comes a breaking point. I stood back staring at her for a couple of minutes trying to figure out what was it that made me want to just save her from a life of ups and downs. I would just about sell my soul to put a smile on her beautiful face.

I cleared my throat to let her know of my presence, and she quickly turned her back to me. I walked over to the couch sitting right beside her. I turned her to me and began to kiss away her tears. She shuttered under me tilting her chin up she placed a light kiss on my lips. Before I knew it, we were locking lips, our tongues were intertwined, and the moans that we both were making with the sound of my heartbeat in my ears were like the beginning of a love song. I pulled away quickly standing up and going in my pocket to pull out the little envelope the doctor gave me with her pills and handed one to her. Her expression was one of bewilderment before she sat up grabbed the glass of water in front of her and swallowed the pill.

Her lips were the softest that I've ever kissed in my life. I went into my bedroom to collect my thoughts. The bulge I had was evidence that the blood that usually gives me a functioning brain was in my pants. What the hell was I thinking her doing this was a cry for help? I didn't feel like I was making this situation any better. Then I imagined her on her knees with her back arched in front of me as I took her from behind, and I hardened more. The taste of her mouth was the sweetest thing I've ever tasted, and I wondered what the rest of her would taste like. I licked my lips just imagining her on my tongue. This girl was going to be the death of me. I rubbed my hand down my shaft quickly realizing I had to go back to her and fix whatever we had going on.

"Damn!" The explosive left my mouth as I raked my fingers through my short hair.

REIGN

What was I thinking? I don't know exactly what came over me when I assaulted Brenton with my mouth. On second thought, yes I did. Today has been one of the worse for me. I have felt numb since I looked into my bank account. Then with a fake picture of me going viral, I needed to feel something. The emotionless state I'm in just isn't working for me. Since I've woken up on his couch, I felt like I was in a daze, and it was time for me to come out of it. What better way to do that than to be under a man that has wanted me since the first day we met. Instead of getting the reaction I wanted, he turned me down and now all I feel is shame. I guess that's better than feeling nothing. These last few weeks have been hell on me, and I was truly tired of crying. I held my head in my hand with my eyes closed trying to figure everything out. I really don't know where I'm going from here.

"I wasn't rejecting you, Reign," Brenton stated.

I didn't even want to look at him, I pitied myself right now, and I couldn't take seeing it in his eyes too. He came and sat next to me, putting his index finger under my chin lifting my head so that he could look into my eyes. I was unsure of the emotion that lingered in his eyes, so I did everything I could not to stare into them.

REIGN

"I'm sorry, Brenton. I can tell you don't like me anymore, and if you want me to leave, I understand." He placed a hand on each side of my face wanting my undivided attention.

"It's not that I don't like you. The problem is that I like you too much to do something that you will regret later. You are going through a lot right now, and I refuse to be your moment of weakness."

I was baffled. This couldn't be the same man that I met a couple of months ago that wanted my body on a platter on top of the table. I stayed mute for a minute to ponder what he was saying.

"What are you saying, Brenton?" I searched his multicolor eyes for an understanding.

For the first time, I really studied the starburst of gray, blue, hazel, and green in his eyes with admiration. This man is beautiful. He had to the epitome of men everywhere. His eyes alone mesmerized me.

"I want more," he stated seriously.

"I'm sorry, more of what?" I quizzed. I blinked my eyes a couple of times to end the spell that I was trapped in. Brenton furrowed his brows at me as if I had just had another little episode in front of him.

"As harsh as this may sound, I can get pussy from anywhere, but what I can't get from other women that you and I have is chemistry and companionship. For the first time in my life, I want more than sex."

He stopped taking a deep breath as if he really didn't know what to say. He got up pacing the floor and pulling at his hair, and my eyes stayed glued to him as he walked back over to me. He took another breath kneeling in front of me.

"I want you. I want all of you and everything that comes along with you." He waited for me to respond, but I was in awe of what he just revealed to me.

"I really didn't want to put all of this on you, especially with everything that has been going on with you. I would have rather waited until you were in a better head space, but with what happened I couldn't." My mouth dropped open a little as I processed what he was saying, but words were failing me.

"You don't have to answer now just think about it," he continued then bit down on his lip out of nervousness.

Brenton took my hand in his pulling it up to his mouth and kissed my palm. This man had the key to every treasure chest I owned. Just that little gesture he did sparked a flame in a certain part of my body. Still holding my hand, he stood up pulling me up with him followed into the bathroom. The shower was running when he opened the door to the bathroom and steam hit us in the face. He led me in the bathroom quickly relieving me of my clothes.

"I'm not going to do anything that you won't allow me to do, but you've had a long day, and I just want to help you relax." I nodded my head at him because I was still lost for words.

He opened the glass to the huge stone shower that was big enough for a family of six. He stripped of all his clothes except his boxer briefs and then got in with me. Before stepping under the water, I took in his medium muscular build and his perfectly tanned skin tone. My eyes roamed over his body and then I trailed my hand over his six-pack. He took in a deep breath, his stomach muscles tightened under my touch, and his manhood started hardening. I gasped and started letting my hands move south, Brenton grabbed my hand.

"If you do that, he might want to you to do other things to make him happy." I lifted my head looking into his eyes, the color of his eyes had darkened and changed.

"I'm sorry. it's just that it's big."

I was awed. Don't get me wrong. I've Googled pictures of penises before, but they were never this big. Maybe it was the fact that I've never seen one up close. I cocked my head really wanting to do some further inspecting.

"Is there something wrong?" he said with a half-smile on his face.

"No, there's nothing wrong," I finally stated turning my back to him, stepping under the rain showerhead.

Brenton pulled me back to him putting shampoo into his hand that smelled like lavender and vanilla. He proceeded to wash my hair gently massaging my scalp. He rinsed and repeated the gesture.

He took some jasmine body wash and washed my back using his

hands to make small circles, and I felt my body relax under his soft but firm touch. He added more of the soap to his hands then pulled me back into his hard body. His cock was hard against my back as he moved his hands to the front of me making those same small circles on my stomach and down my thighs. His touch became hot to my body sending jolts of electricity to my clit causing it to pulsate with need. Once he got to my breasts, he held them in his hands as if he was trying to test the weight of them.

"Perfect," he said in a low tone before he began to knead and massage my breasts.

Stepping forward with me against him, we both were now under the water. Brenton put one hand between my legs and use the other to fondle my nipples. My body was on fire, in need of release, and I wanted so badly for him to give me what I needed. He pulled his hand from my pleasure bud, and I whimpered at the loss of his touch. He turned me to him and began to kiss me slow and sensual taking his time he intertwined my tongue with his.

He moved from my lips and trailed kisses from my mouth to my chest. When he pulled back, I instantly began to miss the heat of his mouth on me. He licked his lips before taking his mouth and gently covering my nipple, while one of his hands was busy fondling my other nipple. This man was turning my body into mush. Brenton licked and suckled my nipple. Moving his mouth to my other breast and paid equal attention to it, he had me squirming under his touch. He began to caress my body with his hands slowly stroking every part of me.

The sensation of his mouth and hands on me sent shivers through my body. My hips began to rotate on their own, and I needed to come. I may be a virgin, but I knew the things my body wanted and needed. Reading my mind, he put one of his hands between my folds. He took one finger penetrating me and used his thumb to rub my pleasure spot as he continued to lavish my nipples with his mouth.

"Please!" I begged, not knowing what I was asking for. The things that he was doing to my body were making me lose control of all my mental functioning. He was taking his time, torturing me with his mouth and hands. He dropped to his knees in front of me.

"Open your legs, baby. Let me taste you." I opened up for him like an obedient child. I was thirsty with need. Brenton looked up into my eyes smirked then attacked my honey pot.

"Oh…my….gosh!" I let out in a pleasurable moan. This is what dreams are made of. Brenton licked my entire yoni with one swipe of the tongue. He pulled away from me.

"Your pussy taste as good as I knew it would." He went back to licking every crevice of me.

"Open up more." I gaped my legs as much as I could without losing my balance in the shower.

Brenton pushed my back flat against the wall and lifted me up a little, putting my legs on his shoulder. He darted his tongue in and out of my opening, and it was driving me crazy. He went back to my clit licking it first slowly then faster. Someway he got a finger inside of my honeypot, and he used his finger to rub on a certain spot inside of me. Whatever he was doing was making me feel so vulnerable, but it felt so good.

My breathing began to increase becoming harsher, and I felt the buildup, I could tell it was going to be the best orgasm that I've ever had in my life. My body shivered and began to tingle from my feet to the top of my head. My body stiffened as I screamed out in sheer pleasure pulling at Brenton's hair. As I began to convulse Brenton kept his finger and mouth on me and in me. My vision began to blur, and I'm sure if I weren't slightly lifted off the floor I would've fallen because my body felt like jelly.

Brenton waited until my shudders stopped. I thought we were done, but no, he rubbed the spot that he had never moved his finger from. Between his mouth and that damn finger, I exploded a second time. This time the orgasm was stronger— I came harder, stars flashed before my eyes, my head began to spin, I felt my eyes cross, and my vision blur completely out.

"FUUUCCCCKKKK!!!" I yelled out as Brenton hummed and

treated my honeydew like it was the best thing he's ever tasted in his life.

He put me on my feet but quickly grabbed me around my waist. He opened the glass grabbing a towel wrapping me up. He cradled me up and walked me into the bedroom placing me on his bed. He lightly kissed my lips, and I could taste the reminiscent of myself on his mouth.

"Try and rest," he told me.

I was lost for words, and my mind was filled with a haziness that I know was there because of him. My body felt so weak and drained that I did the only thing I could and that was to nod my head. Brenton had taken my words, my mind, and my heart. I watched him walk away from me as I drifted off to sleep.

* * *

I woke up feeling overheated and couldn't breathe from the weight of Brenton practically on top of me. I turned my head to the window, and it was dark outside, so I wasn't sure of the time. I tried to move without waking him, so I turned, causing him to slide to the side of me. I tried to get out of the bed, but before I could really move, Brenton's arm snaked around me pulling me closer to him. I felt his breath on the back of my neck right before he placed a feather of kisses there.

"Are you okay?" I could hear the concern in his voice.

"Yes, I just need to go to the bathroom." As soon as the words left my mouth, I saw the passion in his eyes. I could tell he was thinking of everything that we did earlier, and my body flooded with desire.

"You want to take another shower?" Brenton asked me with a smirk on his face. My belly began to stir with need for him. *Couldn't I possibly want more of him after everything we've recently shared?* I asked myself while looking into his eyes.

He used his eyes to caress every place he had touched me, and I became wet with need for him. My womanly parts began to pulsate with me under his gaze. I did the only thing I felt I could do. I got out of the bed going to the bathroom.

He was making me feel things that I didn't know were possible. I washed my hands and reflected on the day that I had, and how I ended up back at Brenton's house. I thought of the things that he did to my body and how just the thought of him cause my girl parts to tighten with need. Every time I saw him, butterflies flutter through my belly. All he's really ever asked me was to let him help me. Right now, I was at rock bottom and had nothing to pull me up, no one but him. I just trusted him with my body, so would I be able to trust him with everything else. I stared at my reflection in the mirror as I continued to wash my hands. I was so used to doing everything by and for myself. Could I drop my guard and let him take control?

BRENTON

She's a virgin, I thought to myself as Reign was in the bathroom. I knew she was a little inexperienced, but a virgin was the last thing to cross my mind. It only made me want to find out who was doing all this to her. I had a feeling it's the same guy that didn't understand it when she told him no.

"I'll accept your offer."

Reign had walked out of the bathroom, and it took me a minute to realize what she was referring to. Once the thought crossed my mind, the smile on my face reflected the happiness I was feeling.

"Was it my expert oral skills that helped you make up your mind?" This time my expression was mischievous as I flicked my tongue at her. The thought of her exquisite taste had my dick hard as bricks.

"Your oral skills are great, but it really has nothing to do with that." Her eyes fell to my boxers and fire blazed in her eyes. I had to find something for us to get into outside of this house or her virginity would be mine for keeps.

"Are you still okay with staying with me for a couple of weeks?" Her eyes finally left my junk and met my eyes.

"Yes, unless you want me to leave." There was a hint of sadness in her voice and eyes.

"I would never tell you to leave. You can stay with me as long as you like."

The joy came back into her eyes before a small smile graced her face, and I felt my dick harden down my leg. I had to get this together, or I'll have blue balls. Reign went and sat on the bed, and I swiftly went to the bathroom.

I turned the shower on and started looking in the cabinet and drawers for some lotion. I hadn't had to use my hand in so long. I literally put the lotion in my hand before stepping into the shower. I leaned back onto the cool stone tile in the shower and thought of Reign and the noises she made as I ate her pussy like it was my favorite meal. I slowly stroked myself as if I would do if I were inside of her. My balls began to twitch and pull up close to my body. I pumped faster until it felt like I was going to burst from the inside out. I grunted as I shot my load onto the stoned floor. I stood there letting the water run down me trying to catch my breath. I stepped out of the shower throwing on some jeans and a t-shirt.

"Let's go to the store to grab you some things for your two-week stay." Reign looked at me.

"I don't have any money," she said sadly.

"Don't worry about it. I will take care of the bill." She arched her eyebrow at me, and I could tell she was ready to protest, so I put my hand up to stop her.

"You said that you would accept my help, so let me do this. Since it's late, we are only going to be able to go to Wal-Mart anyway. I'm sure you need personal items plus, after the long and exciting day, we need some air."

She nodded her head and began to look around for what she had on earlier. I pulled out a pair of my sweatpants and another t-shirt for her. My clothes swallowed her, but the way my pants hung low on hips caught my attention more than anything. I helped her put her curly mass of hair into a huge braid, and we were out the door.

Once in the store for a short while, we stood in the line to check out, and Reign had all of ten items in the cart, I knew I would have to do something about this tomorrow. I didn't want to argue with her, so I let her do what she wanted.

*　*　*

"Brenton... Brenton..." Brenda cleared her throat, getting my attention.

"Yes, Brenda?" I asked and tuned her right back out.

I sat in my office with my mind in the clouds. Reign being at my house was turning out better than I thought it would. When I got home from work yesterday, she had dinner waiting for me. I questioned how she got to the store because the car that I had left the keys to was still in the same spot. She informed me she didn't know how to drive, so she used the money I left to take a cab and get groceries. After dinner, I gave her, her first driving lesson. It started out kind of scary, but she got the hang of it quick.

"Are you listening to me?" Brenda raised her voice.

"I'm sorry what?" I blinked my eyes several times and focused on what she was saying.

"You know what you need a vacation because your attention span has been nonexistent for about a couple of months now." Brenda put her hands on her pudgy waist.

"That's a great idea. Brenda, clear my calendar for the next three weeks and make reservations for a trip to the Dominican Republic." *Does she even have a passport?* I questioned to myself.

"Wait, Brenda. I think I should go somewhere local."

I sat thinking for a minute, Reign was such a down to earth person she wouldn't want me to do too much, and she wouldn't want to go anywhere to flashy.

"Make that Puerto Rico and a trip for two. See if you can get us a flight for tomorrow." Brenda stood in the door. "Is there anything else, Brenda?" I questioned.

"Yes, I came in here to let you know your father has been calling your cell phone for about an hour." She turned and walked away after that. I wasn't interested in whatever my father was calling for, I closed down my computer and got my things together to leave. I needed to take Reign shopping for our trip.

* * *

I WALKED into the house and Reign was dancing around with Beyoncé blasting through the speakers as she used the Swifter Jet on the hardwood floors. She was so into what she was doing that she hadn't noticed my presence. I took my time standing back admiring her moves and enjoying the full view of her behind shaking and belly rolling.

"You know someone comes in to clean the house every other day, right. You don't have to do that." She stopped in the middle of her dance turning to look at me with her mouth gaped.

"Alexa, pause the song." I could tell Reign was a little embarrassed from me interrupting her private show.

"I know, but I was bored. I'm used to going to school and working every day, and I have nothing to do, but sit around."

I took in her appearance in the small shorts that she let me buy her from Wal-Mart. Her butt was practically hanging out of them, and I wanted nothing more than to bite it and trail kisses all over her until I got to her treasure chest. My dick was jumping at the thought of it. I hadn't had the chance to taste her since that day in the shower, and I was more than ready to pounce on her, but I didn't want to touch her again until she was ready.

"Get dressed and let's go out."

She went to the room we were sharing and put some clothes on while I checked my email. Brenda had sent me all of our flight information, and our plane left in three hours. I needed to cancel our shopping trip. We could grab some things while we were in Puerto Rico.

I went into the room to get everything I think we would need. Reign watched me quietly as I made sure I had all of our personal information.

The drive to the airport was quiet. I could tell that Reign was wondering why we were going in the direction of the airport, but she stayed silent and went with the flow.

"Why are we here?" Reign asked as we walked into one of the restaurants. I wanted to make sure she had something on her stomach before we got into the air. The flight was only four hours, but I wasn't sure of the last time she had eaten.

"We're taking a trip," I responded before giving her a quick kiss, ignoring the questioning glare she was giving me.

"Since I have some time off, I thought it would be nice to get out of Boston for a while. You've already taken your finals and school is out for the summer, don't you think it would be nice to just get away for a little while? I watched her ponder what I was saying, and a small smile curved her lips, and I sat mesmerized by her beauty.

"Let's go," she said through her smile, I didn't know I was holding my breath until she said that. I leaned over the table and thoroughly kissed her.

* * *

WE LANDED in Puerto Rico around seven that evening. When we stepped off the plane, I looked into Reign's face and knew I had done the right thing. The beauty of the island fascinated her just like I was enthralled with hers.

"This is so beautiful." As I gazed into her eyes, I wondered if I looked at her the same way she was looking now.

"Just like you," I told her.

"Thank you so much! How long are we staying?" She grabbed my hand as we walked out of the airport.

"As long as you want to," I replied seriously.

"So when I'm ready to leave, we will?" she asked with a smirk on her face. I nodded my head, holding her hand like I never wanted to let her go."

"I'm ready now." She turned me around walking in the opposite direction of the doors. I followed behind her like a lovesick puppy.

"You don't want to stay at least tonight?" I questioned with a hint of sadness in my voice.

She shook her head no, staring up at the signs and navigating us through the crowd. She stopped suddenly, and I bumped into the back of her, then snaked my arm around her to keep her from stumbling to the floor.

"I don't want you to think I expect anything from you while we're here."

I wanted to show her that all men weren't like the asshole that turned her world upside down. I just wanted to spend time with her in a different environment other than my house. Maybe this trip was taking it a little too far. She turned to me looking into my eyes.

"If I haven't learned anything else in the short time that I have been around you, it's that you are not like Bla…" She stopped realizing that she was about to say the name that I had been waiting to hear since that day I found her walking on the side of the road. I raised a brow at her waking for her to finish her statement.

"Not like who?" I asked, expecting her to answer me. She cleared her throat raising up on her tiptoes and kissed me causing my heart to race and me to forget about the subject of the man she was protecting.

"Okay let's see when the next flight leaves out to go home." I secured her hand in mine walking towards the ticket counter.

"I was just joking." She gave me a smile that would make me give up my wealth to keep it permanently on her face. She grabbed my hand, and I made a beeline to the door. I wasn't giving her a chance to change her mind for real.

REIGN

We had been in Paradise for three days, and Brenton was sparing no expense to make me happy. The first night was dinner in our penthouse suit on the balcony, and he introduced me to oysters and caviar just to name a few things. The next day was shopping and parasailing, and today was the spa. I had no idea what we were doing later on tonight, but I knew it was going to be exciting. I was seeing another side of him since most of the time he was very serious. He was showing me that he was charming, caring, and funny. I sat in the chair getting a manicure, pedicure, and my hair done at the same time. My phone went off I picked it up carefully making sure that I didn't mess up my nails.

Brenton: *Meet me in the lobby at seven.*

I shot back a quick okay wondering what the night would bring. I placed a smile on my face just thinking of him.

"That's the smile of a woman that's smitten," an older lady with a thick accent spoke. She was sitting in the chair opposite of me. I thought about what she said for a moment before I spoke.

"I don't know," I stated honestly.

I really liked Brenton, but every time I think that things are going in my favor, something drastic happens. Thinking about where I came from, I knew that I had made it further then what people expected. For that, I was grateful, but the way my life was spiraling out of control, I wasn't sure of my feelings.

"There's no need to think hard about it. The glow that's radiating off you tells it all." She smiled while she stared at me. I felt like she was looking into my soul.

"Mija, you have had a hard life coming up, but you should trust your instincts. Never let what one person does affect your relationship with someone else. Trust what you're feeling."

I didn't say anything. I was kind of freaked out. It was as if she knew I wasn't comfortable with what she was saying, so she didn't say anything else.

Once they were done with my hair and makeup, I stood up looking into the mirror and couldn't believe it was me in the reflection. My eyebrows had been threaded, my makeup was perfect, and my hair— there were no words for it. I was speechless. The older lady looked at me with a huge smile on her face.

"You are beautiful, always remember that."

"Thank you." I smiled at her and started to walk out of the door, but she grabbed my arm.

"Mija, things are looking up for you, but the way to happiness will not be easy. When you feel like everything is crumbling around you, trust in love." I got an uneasy feeling while she spoke. Her hand dropped from me, and I nodded my head at her and swiftly walked to the door.

I got to the penthouse going into the room that Brenton and I shared thinking about what the strange lady had told me.

"Are you here?" I called out. There was a cocktail dress hanging on the outside of the closet door with a note on the nightstand.

I'm getting ready for our night out in another room. Everything that you need is laid out for you. I can't wait to see you tonight.

-Brenton

I READ the note aloud then saw the time, so I pulled my hair up, then took a quick shower. By the time I got ready, I had about ten minutes to spare. I went to the mirror admiring the light pink dress and stilettos that Brenton had picked out for me. The dress wasn't something that I would've picked out for myself, but the edginess of it worked for me. I reapplied the lip gloss that was given to me at the spa, then took a brush stroking it through my hair. I smiled at my reflection and then left the room ready to enjoy my night.

BRENTON

"Oh my fuck!"

Reign had stepped off the elevator, and I wondered how I was going to get through the night with a hard-on. She was gorgeous. The short light pink cocktail dress fitted her like a glove. The day at the spa paid off because she was glowing and her hair. She had straightened her natural curls, and her hair hung down covering the open back of the dress. When she approached me, the distant view hadn't done her justice. Reign smiled at me, and I couldn't help but to kiss her. She pulled me down closer to her, wrapping her arms around my neck.

The moan she let out made me pull away from her. Making noises like that had me wanting to take her back to the room, but I knew she would be against it.

"You look beautiful," I stated, placing my hand in the small of her back and wishing I hadn't. My mind went to all of the ways, and I would rather be touching her right now. I took a deep breath trying to change my train of thoughts.

"How was the spa?" I asked, trying to think of other things above my waist.

"I can't believe you did all this for me. Thank you so much for everything."

I could see the gratitude in her eyes, and it was refreshing. Most of the women I dealt with felt it was their god given right for me to spend my money on them. How much money I had and what I could do for Reign was never an issue because she was the do it yourself type. It felt good being around someone that genuinely appreciated what you did for them.

"I'm glad you enjoyed it," I told her as we got to the club that I was taking her to. I didn't think her smile could get any bigger than it was before, but she proved me wrong. I was falling hard, and I couldn't stop myself from falling.

We walked over to a table in the corner immediately ordering drinks. We both gazed around the club. The energy here was explosive. Reign was sitting in her chair moving to the beat, so I grabbed her hand pulling her to the floor.

"You sure you can keep up with me?" she asked while standing up rolling her hips to the up-tempo music as I led her to the floor.

Once we got in our own space Reign began to wine her hips to the beat, and I stood there perplex at the moves she had. I got behind her leaving a little space between us matching her moves. After dancing for three songs straight, the music switched to something slower, and she started to walk off the dance floor.

"Where are you going?" I grabbed her hand giving it a light tug.

She turned doing a perfect spin causing her hair to fan out before she entered my arms. I wrapped an arm around her waist, and we danced slowly as a woman sang about love in Spanish. The song was fitting. I knew that I felt something stronger than like for her— I was in love. *When did that happen?* I thought to myself. In such a short time she had turned my life upside down. Since the first day I met her, I knew she was different. I knew things with her would be different, but I never knew that I would fall in love. I never thought I could want to do for someone more than I wanted to do for myself. I never thought that I would be a one-woman man. Everything I did now, I thought of her before I did it.

"Who taught you how to dance like this?" I asked her as I tried to pull her closer to me. Her head was lying on my chest. Although physically, the only thing that separated us was clothes, it wasn't close enough. I wanted more of a connection, so I moved her hair and placed my hand on her back.

"I've danced all of my life, but I went to school with Hispanics, and they taught me a lot of their dances. Plus I took dance in school so I can do different types of formal dances as well," she replied then licked her lips, causing my penis to stir and harden against her. She made an O shape with her mouth that didn't make it much better.

I pulled her closer to me sliding my hand down her back grabbing a hand full of her ample behind. She rotated her hips grinding into me then gave me a little flirty smile. I don't know if she realized how much she was playing with fire. I cleared my throat breaking away from her, and instantly felt like I lost a part of myself. I placed my hand in the small of her back walking her back to our table.

"You're not too bad on your feet, I would ask you where did you learn how to do that, but I'm sure you took dance courses growing up." She smirked at me.

"Growing up my family threw a lot of parties and balls. My parents were separated at the time, so from the age of eight when men weren't twirling my mother around the floor, she would twirl me. As I got older, I noticed that women love a man that could dance, so I practiced." With dancing, women were just like men. They loved to imagine what you could do to them in the bedroom."

"So you're an only child?" I smiled at the question.

"No, I have a brother. He goes to Harvard and will be graduating next semester." My brother and I was the best thing that came from my father.

"What about your parents?" I exhaled a breath.

"My mother is great. You're going to love her. My father, on the other hand, well I'm going to keep you far away from him. You'll love my brother too. He's funny.

"Are you and your brother close?" I thought about that before I answered her.

"We're not as close as we used to be before I began my company we were as close as brothers could be. In the beginning, I had to invest a lot of time to get it up and running, so that kind of put a halt to us spending time together. Now that he's in college with sports and being a part of a fraternity, he barely has time. We try to meet up at least once every month or so."

I watched her as she listened intently to what I was saying.

"What about you? I know about your mother, but do you have anyone else family wise?" She had told me a little about herself, but I wanted to know everything about her.

"I have no family. Amber is the closest thing I have to a sister." I briefly saw a wave of sadness flash in her eyes.

"Now you have Amber and me. I'll be your family." Her eyes misted, but not with sadness this time.

"Don't make promises you can't keep," she said barely above the music.

I took her hand so that we could leave. Once we stepped into the warm breeze, I pulled her into my arms bent down placed my lips on hers and kissed her until she moaned in my mouth.

"I don't make promises that I can't keep. I don't know if you noticed it yet, but I'm not going anywhere."

I kissed her again, but this time it was slower with as much passion as I could muster up. I needed her to understand that I was here to stay. She began to let her hands roam slowly over my body. She moved her hands under my shirt letting her fingers go over my six-pack. I inhaled a breath, but never took my lips off hers. She let her hands drop to my now hard cock, and she stroked down it over my pants. I pulled away from her. She had me wanting to bend her over right there in front of the club. She looked at me, and I saw the passion in her eyes.

"Let's go." I pulled her close to me wrapping my arm around her. I had to get the smaller me together before we got back to the room and I stripped all of her clothes off her.

When we entered the room, Reign wasted no time pulling me down to her placing a hot and heavy kiss on me. I intertwined my fingers in her hair. Pulling it a little, she gave me the moan that I had come to love. Rubbing her back, I used one of my hands to unzip the top of her dress causing it to fall to the floor revealing her breasts. I trailed kisses down to the right one sucking hard on her nipple.

"Brenton," she gasped my name out, and it was like music to my ears.

I used my other hand to pull the dress completely off her. I pulled back to look at her, and just when I thought my dick couldn't get any harder, she proved me wrong. I stared at Reign standing before me in a lace white thong that barely covered her and silver stilettos. Her hair was a tangled mess, and her pouty lips were swollen from being thoroughly kissed. I picked her up, and she instantly wrapped her legs around my waist.

"I'm ready," she whispered in my ear before nibbling on it and moving to kiss my neck. She was going to be the death of me.

I got us to the bedroom part of our suite and placed her on her feet. She began to unbutton my shirt. She placed a flutter of kisses on my mouth then deepened it. When her hands wrapped around my dick, I was sure I was about to cum in her hands. She had unbuttoned my pants and held me in her hands. She looked up at me licked her lips, and I almost convulsed on the spot. Reign got on her knees in front of me.

"You don't have to do this," I felt the need to say. I wanted it. I mean I really wanted it, but I couldn't ask her to do this.

"I want to," was her response before she used her hand to stroke me. My eyes rolled in the back of my head just thinking about what she was about to do. Once her warm wet mouth wrapped around the tip of me, I knew I was in for a rude awakening. I had to stop her.

"Reign, what do you want from me tonight? Because if you do this, I won't be able to do anything else so think about this hard." She still held me in her hands and hadn't stopped stroking me. I was so tempted to toss her on the bed and bury myself into her.

"We have time," she stated before placing her mouth back on me, causing me to go weak.

She twirled her tongue around the head of my penis then made half of it disappear right before my eyes. I closed my eyes because if I watched her, I wouldn't last long at all. She stroked me up and down with her hand. I was so close to the edge I couldn't take any more. I was about to come, so I wrapped my hands in her hair trying to pull her back.

"Stop baby. I don't want to come in your mouth."

She kept going locking her lips tighter sucking harder. I pulled her hair harder this time, but she was relentless. She moaned with pleasure as I pulled at her hair and that sent me over the edge. When I saw her swallow, my knees buckled, and she looked at me innocently.

"Was it okay?" she asked so unsure of herself. I took a deep breath, dropping to my knees in front of her.

"It was the best," I responded before kissing her long and hard.

REIGN

Brenton's taste was still fresh in my mouth when he placed his lips on mine. He pulled back looking into my eyes. His multicolored eyes darkened right before me, and it was almost as if the colors rearranged themselves, causing me to get a little dizzy. He scooped me up off the floor carefully placing me on the bed. He took my heels off my feet and kissed each one of my toes then let my big toe disappear in his mouth. He trailed kisses up my legs skipping my middle. He caressed my body where his lips hadn't landed. He paid special attention to my breasts sucking, kneading, and licking them. He found spots behind my ear and on my neck that made me wiggle underneath him. He was sending surges of heat all through my body just with his hands and mouth.

He fingered me, rubbing that special spot he found days ago watching me come apart on his fingers. Brenton was worshiping and lavishing my body like I was the only woman he wanted in this world. He was driving me crazy, but when he went down on me, it was unexplainable. I came harder than I had in the shower. I was panting, and my body was still burning wanting more of him. I needed him inside of me.

"I need more. I'm ready, Brenton."

He paused above me pondering what I said to him. I could tell although he wanted and needed more too, he was about to tell me no. I placed my hand between us grabbing his hard, huge length and stroked him. I knew what I wanted, and he was going to give it to me. Brenton growled low, and I quickly sat up swallowing his growl with my mouth. I put my hand under the pillow getting the little gold packet that he kept under there. I ripped it open with my teeth.

"Help me put it on," I demanded. He opened his eyes long enough to grab my hands helping me roll it over him.

"Lay back," he told me intertwining my tongue with his as he started back over my breasts and fingering me. Once my juices were dripping off his fingers, he placed the head of his penis at my entrance very slowly moving inside of me.

"Ohh!" I cried out from the pain and pressure of my body accepting him.

"I can stop at any time baby, just let me know," Brenton said through gritted teeth as he paused pulling out of me.

"No please don't," I begged.

He entered me slowly again pulling out and going back in. The pain was starting to be more than I could bear, but I wanted this. I closed my eyes tight digging my nails into the skin on is back.

"Open your eyes and look at me." I looked into his eyes and saw many emotions swarming in his eyes.

"This is going to hurt Reign, but only for a minute. Before I go too far, are you sure?" I nodded my head at him then closed my eyes.

"I need to hear it, baby." I opened my eyes seeing sweat beading on his face.

"Yes," I told him, keeping my eyes on his.

Each time that he had pulled out of me, he went in just a little deeper. He pulled out going back in, and I felt the barrier that was keeping him out rip. I opened my mouth to scream only for him to cover my mouth and swallow it. He stilled inside of me letting me adjust to his size. Once I thought I was adjusted to him, he moved and added a little more of himself into me.

"How much more of you is left?" I asked, starting to feel like I was overfilled with him.

"Just a little more baby, give me a second." I held my breath waiting for the rest of him to enter me. He began to move, the pain began to subside for pleasure, and my body began to adjust to all of him.

"You feel so good, baby."

"Yes," I answered.

Brenton bent down covering my nipple with his mouth causing my stomach muscles to tightened I felt my muscles squeeze him from below. He continued to assault me with his mouth and penis at the same time. This time the urge I felt to come was different. It was stronger, and it was harder. My entire body heated then spasmed. I exploded with Brenton's name on my tongue. He picked up speed with his hands tangled in my hair, pulling my head to the side. Oh my god, another one was coming.

"Reign."

"Brenton."

We called each other's name simultaneously, and I exploded again feeling the wetness leaving my body. He slumped down on his elbows swiftly turning on his back pulling me on top of him.

"Are you okay?" he asked, sounding as exhausted as he looked.

"I'm more than okay," I stated before kissing his lips, and he wrapped his arms around me. My honeypot clenched down again, causing us both to exhale. I tried to move, but Brenton held me tight.

"No, don't move yet, just let me stay connected to you." I nodded my head on his chest as he pulled me tighter to him. We laid in silence as I let his heartbeat become the lullaby that put me to sleep.

* * *

"You're looking good," Amber told me as she hugged me tightly. I had missed her and was happy to be back at work.

We had been back in Boston for two weeks now, but as soon as I got back, I checked in with the doctor that had come to see me and started therapy. It had actually helped for me just to talk things out with a complete stranger. I'm not saying that everything is excellent in my life, but I'm trying to take it in that direction.

"I missed you so much." I tightened the hug on my only friend.

"How was your trip?" she asked. I smiled so hard at her my cheeks began to hurt.

"From that smile, I guess we can say it went good."

I had so much to fill her in on. I hurried to change into my uniform so that I could start my shift. Of course, Brenton stressed to me that I didn't have to work, but I needed to. I had worked all my life, so the six figures in my new account weren't going to stop me. Plus, I knew better than anyone that the money could disappear in the blink of an eye.

"I love him." Her mouth dropped open, and for the first time, my friend was speechless.

"I don't know what to say," she finally spoke. Her mouth dropped open once more then closed. Then I saw it, she was trying to hide it, but her emotions played across her face. First, it was shock, next excitement, then concern.

"Reign, I just don't want you to get hurt. I know that you agreed to go with him to the gala, I understand that part, but love?" she questioned. I didn't want to go back and forth with my only friend about my feelings.

"Don't worry, Amber. He is everything that we never expected him to be. I know he came off as the player type, but he's so much more than that." I thought about everything that we had done together and about how he takes care of me. My body shivered at the thought of his touch.

"From the look on your face, I can tell that you care about him a lot, just be careful. Men like him don't change overnight." My body stiffened.

"You should know since you were so adamant about Blake and me getting together. We both know how that tragedy ended."

I stared her down then regretted the words as soon as they left my mouth. I didn't want to fight with my friend, especially when she only had my best interest at heart. I let my eyes roam the room because I couldn't look at the hurt on her face. This was wrong. I was wrong.

"I'm sorry, I know you are only worried about me and how this would turn out, but Brenton will never intentionally hurt me." I gave her a hug holding on a little longer than usual, and she held on to me just as long as I held on to her.

"Let's get to work," was her reply.

Once we released each other, I walked behind her on to the floor with my man on my mind. Could I really call him that? Was he my man? The questions that I began to ask myself took me into a whirlwind of more questions. How could I be in love with someone and didn't know what our relationship consist of? Amber may have been right about this.

"Are you okay?" Dennis had a worried expression on his face. I would stare at me the same way if my last memory of myself were practically having a nervous breakdown. I cleared my throat to overcome the shock.

"I'm fine, Dennis." I pulled a towel out and started wiping the bar. I had to keep busy under his appraisal of me.

"Good to have you back," he said before walking away from me. I stopped cleaning the bar and walked away to wait my tables.

Two Weeks Later

Today we had to attend the gala, and I was a ball of nerves. Although Brenton had sent me to the spa earlier in the day, I was still on edge. We had been in San Antonio Texas for three days, and the city was beautiful. We had been, horseback riding, swimming, shopping, and out to dinner these last couple of days. Once I opened a new account with another bank, Brenton put six figures into my account. As much as I protested and begged him to take the money back, he refused. I even went to the bank took seventy thousand out, went back to the house and demanded Brenton take it back. To my surprise he did, and I was relieved. I slept great that night only to wake up the next morning with an extra one hundred forty grand in there. That was his way of telling me he can do what he wants. I quickly learned that it's best to leave well enough alone when it concerns money.

"Are you ready, babe?" Brenton asked me as he walked into the bedroom that we shared at the Ritz Carlton.

"Almost, I just need some help with the zipper on the gown." He casually walked over to me waiting for me to put on the earrings that he picked out. The more I stared at them, I was sure they were diamonds, but I knew better than to broach the subject with him.

"Did I tell you how beautiful you look?" I smiled watching his reflection in the mirror as he slowly zipped my dress. He placed kisses on my back. As he completed his job, heat spread through me from his soft kisses.

"Yes, you have and thank you again," I replied curtly. Now not only was I nervous, but my body was craving his touch in more than one place. I couldn't get enough of him, and every time he stepped into a room, I wanted him inside of me in a way that I couldn't describe.

"Don't be nervous, Reign. Everyone here will love you, and my grandfather and mother will adore you. You're intelligent, funny, beautiful, and so kind-hearted that the angels are jealous. Plus, it doesn't matter what anyone else thinks of you because I love you."

He placed a kiss behind my ear then froze. I stared at his expression in the mirror, was it too soon for us to say that word? I knew that I loved him just as much if not more than he loved me. We hadn't even talked about being in a relationship, but he loved me. I began to see the panic in his eyes along with regret.

"I love you too!" I swallowed, not sure of how to act after letting him know how I felt. I know he had just said it to me, but I was still scared for some reason. Do I kiss him now or what? He stared into my eyes through our reflection as if he was trying to pierce through my soul to find out my deepest darkest secrets.

"I'm sorry, I can tell now that you were just caught in the moment, and it slipped from your mouth. We should just finish this night out, and we can go back to the way that it was before," the words stumbled out of my mouth. I felt rejected by him for the second time since we've been around each other. "I mean we are not even a couple, so I get it."

For some reason I had to keep talking, I feel like I was talking to myself more than I was talking to him. It was like I had to say it out loud so that I could clear my mind of the fairytale he had enveloped me in. Brenton kissed my shoulder. Turning me to him, he began to kiss me slowly then deepened the kiss. It was as if he was pouring himself into me, trying to kiss away all the doubt that was running through my brain at his silence. He pulled me closer to him like he was trying to make us one mind, body, and soul. Grabbing my butt, he lifted me off my feet and my legs wrapped around him as if they belonged there. I was so spent when he finally broke the kiss that when he put me back on my feet, I was dizzy. We both were breathing hard staring at each other.

"If you had any doubt about how I feel, I hope that reassured you. As much as we had been together lately, I didn't think I had to tell you that we are a couple. I do love you, and I'm glad to know that you feel the same way." He grabbed me around the waist and placed a quick kiss on my lips. I nodded my head at him because I was still high off love and the kiss we had just shared.

He walked out of the room, and I faced the mirror seeing swollen lips and a few strands of hair had fallen from my chignon. I swiftly fixed my hair and reapplied my lipstick stepping out into the living area. Brenton took my hand as we walked to the elevator. Once we got outside, there was a white limousine waiting for us. We had a short silent ride to his grandfather's estate, and Brenton held my hand the entire way there. I became more relaxed about being there with him and meeting his family. I knew as long as he was by my side that I would be able to calmly make it through the night.

"This house is beautiful," I told Brenton as we walked in the door. We went to a ballroom that was decorated with silver and black everywhere. I had truly never even dreamed of something so beautiful. There were ice sculptures, crystal chandeliers, waiters and waitresses dressed in black and silver carrying champagne, wine, and other assorted drinks and beverages. There was a band on a makeshift stage that was playing and singing. I was awed by everything I was seeing.

"I'm glad you decided to bring a date."

I think Brenton and I both stiffened from the voice at the same time. I had only heard this voice once in my life, but I knew who it belonged to. Brenton turned with me holding tightly to his arm. I guess rich people run in the same circles. I placed a tight smile on my face.

"Andrew," Brenton said, nodding his head a little.

"I would ask you to introduce me to your date, but I have already had the pleasure." Mr. Prescott's eyes raked over me, and my skin started to crawl.

"Mr. Prescott," I said with a hint of disdain in my voice. Brenton stiffened again. The tension between us was thick.

"So you're running around using grandfather's last name? I knew all along that my mother wore the pants in the house, but how much bitch can one man have in them?"

I snickered at his statement then cleared my throat.

"Reign, this is my dad Andrew Thomas."

What in the holy hell was going on here? I looked from Brenton to Andrew and damn near fell out. Four pairs of multicolored eyes roamed over me. Fuck my life; they were practically twins. Brenton looked just like this man. Why didn't I figure this out? I searched my mind trying to see if I had missed something along the way. Brenton didn't have a picture of his family in his house. Well, I could understand not having one of his dad. The man was an asshole. He also had no pictures of his mother or Blake either. I pinched myself to make sure I wasn't having a nightmare.

"I see you and your brother have the *exact* same taste in women." He put emphasis on the word exact. I looked between them again. This could not be happening. Am I having a nightmare or is this the twilight zone? I held my breath closed my eyes then opened them back up.

"What the hell is that supposed to mean?" Brenton puffed his chest out, and I could tell that he was more than upset.

You could feel the tension between them, but when Andrew came a little closer to Brenton, I knew it was about to be a problem. While the men stared each other down, I could see the steam coming off Brenton. He was just that angry. I put a hand to Brenton's chest stopping him from being nose to nose with his father.

"Are you starting with my grandson already, Andrew?" A silver-headed, tall man walked up to us. His attire was immaculate. I took in his height, build, and eyes. Blake resembled him a lot. I looked between the three men watching the smirk that graced Andrew's face.

"I would never, Mr. Prescott," he lied smoothly then turned to walk away from us.

I was grateful, but after finding out who Brenton's father was, I had a lot of explaining to do, but would Brenton believe me when I tell him about what his brother tried to do to me.

"This is my grandfather Brad Prescott, grandfather this is Reign," Brenton introduced us, and Mr. Prescott smiled at me so big that it put my heart at ease. Although he was old, his eyes were full of youth and excitement. Mr. Prescott grabbed my hand bringing it to his mouth kissing the palm of it. I instantly knew that Brenton spent a lot of time with him.

"It's a pleasure to meet the woman that Benny here has been raving about for months. I can see why he's head over heels for you. You are beautiful, and before we go any further, please call me Grandfather or Brad." I smiled. This old man was a charmer and down to earth. I knew I would be putty in his hands in no time.

"The pleasure's all mine." I avoided calling him anything because I wasn't sure how long I would be around the family after talking to Brenton.

"I have to go greet the rest of the guests. Save a dance for me, Reign." I nodded my head as Mr. Prescott walked in the directions of the double doors. Brenton pulled me into his arms placing a kiss on my forehead.

"I'm sorry about my dad," he whispered in my ear as he swayed with me.

"I have to tell you something?" He kissed my lips.

"Later, let's get through the night, and we'll talk later."

The ball of nerves was back with a vengeance and wasn't letting up. I have a feeling tonight is going to be a disaster, and I will be right smack in the middle of it. I took a deep breath trying to calm my nerves, but it wasn't working. I saw Blake and his father talking in the corner, Andrew pointed out Brenton and me. I laid my head on Brenton's chest trying to ignore them, but Brenton felt the tension in me.

"Come with me." He pulled me off the dance floor, and we walked pass everyone going through a door that led through the kitchen. We went up the stairs, and when we got to the door, he paused then opened it.

"Where are we?" I asked looking around the room admiring the gray and white furniture that took up very little space in the room.

"This is my bedroom. When I was little, I spent a lot of time on the estate with my grandfather. My mother and Andrew had gone through a huge breakup, my mother shut down for a while, and Grandfather Prescott took care of me." I couldn't place the emotions that crossed in his eyes, but it made me want to hold him close, so I did.

"We need to talk, Brenton. It's important," I stated before I let him go. He kissed my lips slowly. I followed his lead, and then he deepened the kiss. Our tongues intertwined and played a game of tug of war as we tried to outkiss each other. He pulled away from me.

"No, you need to relax."

My dress hit the floor in a pool around my feet. I was so into the kiss that I hadn't noticed him unzipping my dress. I stepped over my dress holding it up so it wouldn't wrinkle.

"We can't do this here. Your grandfather is having a party downstairs." My eyes were wide as I saw the predatory expression on his face. My heart was about to explode with the love I had for him, and at that moment, I knew I would do anything that this man asked me to do.

I watched him take off his jacket cufflinks and shirt. He laid our clothing across a chair so that they wouldn't wrinkle, and then he looked at me licking his lips. My body was on fire, and I was sure the thong that I had on could be wrung out I was so wet. I swallowed as I stood there looking at the man that I loved, and the man that I was sure I would be losing tonight. I would give him anything in the world that he asked me for.

Brenton pulled a nipple in his mouth and rolled the other one between his fingers. I let out a small sigh as he lavished me. Keeping his mouth on me, he walked me backwards until my bottom hit the bed. Putting a finger between my slippery folds, he sunk two deep into me rubbing the spot that he discovered so well. He took his thumb and began to rub my clit.

"Roll on it, Reign. Act like my dick is inside of you and you want to come all over it. Give me what I want baby and what you need."

I found my body following his command as my hips lifted off the bed and began to rotate at his will. He put his mouth back on my breast causing me to cry out in pleasure. He moved down and replaced his tongue with his thumb, and I fell apart right then. The flood that left my body made me weak. Brenton pulled me closer to him kissing my cheek. We laid with him just holding me for a minute, before he got up.

"Let's go back out." He pulled me out of bed, helping me step into my dress before putting on his own clothes. To my surprise, I felt much better.

BRENTON

"I've been looking for you. It's time for dinner." My brother Blake had caught me by the arm coming from the restroom.

"Okay, I have to get my date, and then I'll be right over."

Blake walked off going back into the ballroom. Reign came out, and we went over to our family table at the front of the room. My grandfather and brother stood once we walked up, but my dad stayed in his seat. When my brother's eyes met Reign's, I knew it was something. Fear crossed his eyes then disdain.

"Nice seeing you again, Reign," my mother said like she was relieved to see her.

"It's nice seeing you again too, Julie. How have you been?" Reign asked my mother. I looked over to my grandfather like he had all the answers and he shrugged his shoulders at me.

"How do you all know, Reign?" I nailed all of them with my eyes except my grandfather.

"Evidently you and your brother like the same whores." I stared my dad down, and I wanted to kill him for talking about Reign like that. It wasn't like I expected more from him, but did he have to be such an asshole.

YASAUNI

"Watch your mouth, Andrew," my mother spoke up before I could.

"I will have none of this at this gala. We will talk about this later once everyone leaves. By the way, Andrew, watch how you address the women population under my roof," my grandfather said through his teeth.

"Yes, sir, Mr. Prescott," my dad answered I shook my head, things would never change.

Blake flagged down one of the waiters and got two glasses of whiskey off the tray. He drank one quickly then sipped the other. My mother was sitting there looking like she was holding on to someone's darkest secret, and my dad was looking at everything except me. Reign sat next to me shaking her foot and twisting her hands. What the hell was going on around me? I touched Reign's leg to try and calm her, and she flinched under my touch. Once she realized it was me, she calmed a little.

We sat and ate dinner in silence as everyone around us chattered and had a good time. My grandfather got up going to the microphone.

"Hello everyone, I hope you all are enjoying yourselves tonight." He smiled at everyone as the agreed to him.

"Anyway, you all know that I'm not one to make long speeches, so this will be short and sweet. I know that we all have done great for ourselves with Prescott Oil, and I couldn't have done any of it with any of you."

The crowd clapped, looking around with reverence in their eyes for each other. Grandfather wasn't lying, I have stock in our families company, and I have made a lot of money from it. Grandfather waved his hand for everyone to settle down.

"I'm getting old, and the way I run things is in an old-fashioned way. Yes, that way has been good to us, but I feel we could do great. With that being said, I'm retiring in a year." Everyone gasped. Looking around the table, I mouthed to my mother *did you know this?* She shook her head no to me with the same look that everyone else had on their face.

"Don't fret. I will not leave you without giving you someone that is more than capable of taking my place."

My father had a look of satisfaction on his face as he stood up waiting for my grandfather to call his name. I furrowed my brows at the thought of my grandfather handing our family business over to my dad. Andrew has worked for my grandfather's company for over thirty years, so it wouldn't really surprise me, but then again it would. It's not like it would be too far out of mine and Blake's reach in the future if we wanted to take it over.

"Brenton, come up here son." My grandfather called my name, and my mouth dropped. My mother and Reign was both nudging me to get my attention.

I walked up to the stage with my head in the clouds. I never expected this. My father was giving me an evil eye, and I could tell he was jealous. He has always wanted to take over our family business. He sat down slumping in his chair, but really what did he expect. He was married into the family, not blood.

"My grandson, Brenton Prescott Thomas, will take you all into the next generation. I have no doubt in my mind that you will make a great CEO, Benny."

I stood next to grandfather smiling as everyone stood and clapped for me. Although it was over six hundred people in this room, it was only one face I wanted to see, and that was Reign's. My eyes landed on her on the big smile she was wearing, and I knew that with her by my side I could do anything.

* * *

"Hey Brenton, it's been a long time."

I turned away from the bartender looking into the eyes of Hailey, the first girl that broke my heart. *What the fuck was she doing here?* She never came to these events because she knew it was a chance of running into me.

"Hey, Hailey," I said dryly hoping she would get the hint that I didn't want to be bothered. To be honest, I hated this girl, she was everything any man would fuck, but girlfriend or wife wise, she lacked a few things, like a heart.

"You're not happy to see me?" she asked with her bottom lip poked out in the way I used to like before she slept with my childhood best friend. It happened right before I went to college. Every time I think about it, I still want to beat Gary's ass. She smiled at me like I was her next meal ticket.

"I guess you can tell that from the tone of my voice, huh?" I asked sarcastically.

"That was a long time ago. You should be over it by now, I am." She has a lot of fucking nerve. I closed my eyes to take a deep breath then walked close to her so that no one could hear what I was saying.

"Just because a snake sheds its skin doesn't mean it still isn't a snake. Now get the hell out of my way, I have to go back to my girlfriend." Hailey blocked me in not letting me move and placed a kiss on my lips. I couldn't hit a woman, so I did the next best thing. I bit her tongue.

"Really Brenton?"

I didn't have to turn around. I could envision the hurt on Reign's face as she stood behind me. I closed my eyes not believing this was happening. Hailey took advantage of the situation by wrapping her arms around my waist. I stiffened at her touch.

"Aww, aren't you cute. You thought he would want someone like you when he could have me." I pushed Hailey away from me turning just in time to see the tears in Reign's eyes. She turned her back to me walking away.

"Reign, wait. It's not what you think!" I yelled to her back as she was speed walking through the crowd, I turned back to see Hailey trying to nurse her tongue, but she had a look of satisfaction on her face. If Reign left me because of her, I swear I will blackball her ass.

"Where are you going?" Andrew had wrapped his arms around Reign, and I saw the panic etched on her face.

"Get your fucking hands off of her," I told my dad.

"How did things work out with you and Hailey?" he asked me as he practically pushed Reign into my waiting arms. I pull her to me holding her tight forgetting Andrew's presence. I whispered in Reign's ear letting her know that everything would be okay.

"Stay away from her, Andrew. This is your first and last warning." My dad held a smirk on his face.

"You think you know her? You don't know shit about the little gutter rat." I felt like my insides were about to burst with anger, I took a step towards him and Reign pushed me back.

"Not here, not now, this gala is a celebration for you. Your dad is just mad that you're his boss now and there's nothing he can do about it." I listened to Reign, but we needed to leave. I had to find my grandfather. I took Reign over to my mother and went off to search for the old man.

I found him about ten minutes later talking to some of the investors. They shook my hand and gave me serval pats on the back followed by congratulations.

"Can I speak with you for a minute in private?' I asked my grandfather. He had a worried expression on his face, and I wished I could ease it for him.

I knew I had to get Reign out of here before my father did something to her then I would have to fight him. The last thing I wanted to do was fight my dad, but I would if he disrespected Reign again.

"I hate to rush out of here, but Reign and I are leaving." He nodded his head.

"You've only been here a few hours, and our investors would like to talk to you one on one." I knew what he was saying was true, but after the stuff with Hailey and Andrew, I needed to get Reign as far away as possible.

"I will stay in town for a couple more days to speak with all of them, but I have to leave now." We shook hands, and I was about to make my way back to Reign when someone tapped the microphone.

Can I have everyone's attention?" a drunken Blake said over the mic.

"There's someone here that doesn't belong." He pointed to where Reign and my mother was.

"Shit!" my grandfather and I said at the same time, I started moving through the crowd trying to get to Blake before he said something dumber than he already said.

"This girl right here... wave to everyone, Reign." Everyone's eyes fell on Reign as Blake continued.

"She's nothing but a waste of the oxygen we breathe. My dad told me that girls like her are meant for one thing. He told me I couldn't love her because she's a whore and only wants my money. He also said that they run in packs like wolves. She must be in a pack of her own because she has fucked my brother and me. I only wanted to tell the people of our society to watch out for bitches like her. I was smart enough to get away from her and take all the money that I had wasted on her back. My brother wasn't as smart as I was though. Evidently he has taken a liken to her. Brother, I just want you to know that all puppies are cute and cuddly until one day they turn into a vicious dog."

I heard several people gasping as I tried to move faster through the thick crowd they all turned their eyes on Reign. She had tears running down her face, and I wanted to do bodily harm to my brother.

"Say's the rapist," I heard Reign say, and my body went stiff.

I saw her moving out of the corner of my eye I couldn't chase her, I was furious, and Blake would pay for this. I made it to the stage and landed a hard blow to my brother's jaw. He was the reason she was going through all this shit, and I would make him pay for it all. She didn't deserve the shit he put her through. No one deserved it. All of the memories of her crying and not wanting to tell me what happened to her flooded my mind, and I unleashed it all on Blake.

"You did this to her, how could you?" I yelled as someone pulled me off my brother. At that time, he got up and landed a hard blow to my eye and stomach. I pulled away from them and attacked Blake again being pulled off once more.

"Stay the fuck away from her. If you do anything else to her, I will forget you're my brother." I snatched away from the people that were holding looking around the room for Reign she was nowhere in sight.

"FUCK!!" I yelled then took off running outside only to see that the limousine was gone and Reign was gone too.

REIGN

I sat in the back of the limousine with tears blurring my vision as I booked a flight. I had to get away from here. I couldn't think straight. My phone rang for the fourth time. It was Brenton, but I couldn't talk to him right now. I never wanted to hear the things that I knew would come out of his mouth. I wasn't ready to face him having accusations in his eyes. I couldn't do it. I know that he would believe his brother over me. He had just told me how close they were. Even though his brother is an asshole, I wouldn't want to be responsible for messing up their family. I took the pins out of my hair that was holding my chignon in place letting my hair drop.

I had gotten so caught up in the world that Brenton had introduced me to only to be torn down and embarrassed in front of damn near one thousand people.

We pulled up to the airport, and I wiped the tears from my face. I couldn't let people see me like this. I was a mess my eyes were puffy and red, so I pulled out a pair of sunglasses that was in my purse and put them on my face. So what it was dark outside, I needed to hide the pain that was etched on my face. I boarded the plane to Chicago and left everything that was Brenton behind me.

* * *

I HELD up in a hotel in downtown Chicago for three days, and I cried until the tears stopped falling. I had to rid myself of the world that Brenton had created for me. This was no longer a fairytale, and I had to get back to reality, my reality. What better way than to do that is walk through my old neighborhood and stop by Queenie's grave. I think it's so crazy that I can walk the streets of one of the most dangerous places in the United States and feel so comfortable, free, and safe.

I sat down on Queenie's grave and just thought for a minute.

"Hey ma, I know it's been a long time, but I was only doing what you told me to do when I was younger. I was going to school and working hard. You always instilled in me to go to school, get good grades, and become someone important. Out of everything you told me you never told me about love, you never told me to watch out and not get my heart broken." I choked on my words.

I put my hand on the grass and started rubbing my hand over it before I continued.

"I feel cheated, Queenie. You left me without warning and with no one there to pick up the pieces. I'm doing great in school, but I'm horrible at real life. I was almost raped."

I raised my voice, the tears were falling steadily now, and the more I wiped my face, the more the tears fell.

"I found the guy of my dreams only for him to be my attempted rapist's brother, and let's not get on his father. These are the times that I need you to hold my hand, and there is no one here to do that. I have no one, and the shit hurts, ma. You left me."

"You have me," Brenton's voice spoke softly from behind me. I turned to see him standing right in front of me looking like a dream come true.

"How did you find me?" I asked turning my back on him. He was invading a private conversation between my mother and me.

"I hired a private investigator when you didn't go home," he replied. I continued to stare at my mother's headstone.

"You found me. I'm okay. Now you can go," I stated without looking at him.

"I'm leaving when you do." He came and sat next to me, the warmth from his body immediately made me hot.

"I promised you that we would talk later, now is later. So what happened between you and my family?" he casually asked as if his brother hadn't already told him. I raised my eyebrow looking at him

"Haven't they told you already?"

"Not really, my brother said you were wild and fucked anything that moves, but I knew that wasn't true. I have a feeling the day I saw you walking up the road you were leaving from my family's house."

I sat quietly for what seemed like hours before I told him what happened that night he found me. It was really only one good thing I could say about that night, and that was that he found me.

"When you left me, it felt like you took all my air with you, and I couldn't breathe. I never want to feel that again in my life."

Everything that he was telling me was what I was feeling. When I left and swore I would never talk to or see him again, my heart fell in pieces. I had sworn off him and other men.

"I know the feeling. You mean so much to me, and if we broke up forever, I don't know if I would be able to take it," I told him seriously. He has brought so much joy into my life that I know that without him I'm nothing. My heart only beats for him, and if he's not there to make it pump, I will die.

"Well, how about we never leave each other again and to make sure of it how about we take a vowel until death do us part."

Brenton pulled out a ring picking up my hand placing a kiss in my palm before sliding a five-carat, princess cut, diamond platinum ring on my finger. I sat there shocked with my mouth open. Brenton patiently waited for me to answer him. I stared into the ring then at him, and I finally closed my mouth.

"Yes!" I whispered before tossing myself into his arms and kissing him. Yet again, tears were rolling down my face, but I guess it was okay because these are happy tears. Brenton had made me the happiest woman on this earth.

REIGN

ONE YEAR LATER

Here we were back in San Antonio, Texas. Brenton had been splitting his time between his own company and Prescott Oil. Things seemed to be looking up for us, and it was about time. Instead of having the Prescott Gala this weekend, Brenton and I were having the wedding of our dreams.

"Just in case you want to run for it at the last minute, my car is running in the front of the door," my best friend and maid of honor Amber said.

"I'm sorry I can't let you two do that. Even if I wanted to, Brenton would kill me," Dennis told us with laughter in his voice.

Dennis stared at Amber with a sparkle in his eyes, I knew he was sweet on her, but for some reason, he hasn't approached her. Feeling my gaze on him, he looked at me and cleared his throat.

"I'm sorry Reign, but Brenton had me to move the car from the door and park four cars so close to it you wouldn't be able to leave if you wanted to," Brenton's friend Chase informed us. I started laughing. If nothing else, he had some crazy friends, especially Brenton's best friends from college. There was Dennis of course, Dylan, and Chase.

The music started up, and my bridesmaids started moving

forward. It was time. Butterflies fluttered in my stomach at the thought of seeing my future husband. We had come so far and gone through so much that I couldn't wait to have his last name.

It was my turn to walk down the aisle, and I came down the aisle by myself. I had no one to walk me down to the love of my life. Grandfather Prescott had offered, but I needed to do this by myself. I needed this to be a reminder for me. I had been by myself for so long, and I had no one to call family. I couldn't call my mother, and I didn't know who my father was. I had no relatives that I knew of, which left me lonely most of the time. It was okay for what it was, but now I had something to look forward to and someone that would be by my side, that I could wake up to in the morning and go to bed at night with. I did this walk down the aisle by myself because I knew from this day forward I would never be alone.

Brenton

WATCHING Reign walk down the aisle to me was a dream come true. I couldn't keep my eyes off her. She was just that beautiful. I turned towards my mother. She and my grandfather were standing together holding hands watching my love walk down the aisle to me. My dad and brother hadn't been invited to the wedding. I still couldn't believe that Blake tried to rape Reign. I knew that everything Blake had said about Reign at the gala was a lie. She couldn't possibly be that much of a hoe when her first time was with me. I discovered with the help of some of his friends that Reign's bank account had been compromised. I was ready to beat them all for doing this, but my future wife didn't want any problems while she finished school. Although I assured her several times nothing would happen to her, she still wouldn't let me do anything. This woman was truly a saint, and I loved her more for that.

Once Reign got to the front next to me, I pulled her to me kissing her long and soft until grandfather cleared his throat.

"Wait until the honeymoon, son. You'll have plenty of time to do as you please with her." He gave me a solid smile, and I let the priest start the ceremony.

"I, Brenton Prescott Thomas, take you, Reign Davis, to be my lawfully wed wife."

The End

Continue reading for a preview of my next release of BWWM romance…

AMBERS BURNING: A TWIST OF FATE

Amber

Oh my gosh, my head is pounding, I thought to myself. I didn't want to open my eyes for fear of my head exploding. *Why did I do this to myself, and where the hell am I?* I laid with my eyes closed for what seemed like an hour trying to avoid the inevitable. I thought back to last night's festivities, trying to see exactly where I went wrong, and then I heard a groan next to me. It was someone else here. I stiffened, about to go into panic mode when a huge arm came around my tiny waist pulling me close to him. The smell of his cologne hit my nose, and I instantly relaxed in his arms, until I realized we shouldn't have been here. I jumped out of bed trying to ignore the pain that was slicing through my head.

"What happened?" a shocked sleepy deep voice asked me with his eyes closed.

"I have no idea Dennis," I lied I knew exactly what happened, well not all of the particulars, but I knew we ended our night with a night of drunken passion.

Flashes of it were coming back to me, but if it hadn't, my body was telling the story. I was stiff and hurting on parts that should never hurt. No, I wasn't a virgin, but it had been a long time. I can't believe this happened. I looked around for something to cover my nudity before Dennis realized who he was talking to and sat up in the bed. I had no such luck.

"Amber!" Dennis all but yelled my name, sitting up and looking at a very naked me.

I can't believe this happened. I turned to look for anything that I could use to cover my body with, but not before I heard his groan. This was different from the other one. This one told me a story of how much Dennis would love to be between the same legs that were stiff with the pain of lovemaking. Not only that but from the sound of this man's groan my body betrayed me, and I felt a flood of wetness leave my body. *I CAN'T BELIEVE THIS IS HAPPENING!* My brain yelled at me this time. *You've already done it, so it shouldn't be a problem if we do it again.*

My body was screaming for Dennis's touch. I turned to look at him, and his dick was as hard as a brick as he looked at me with so much passion in his eyes. My nipples turned into pebbles underneath his gaze, and I let my arms drop because his eyes commanded that I did so. I wanted him so badly but didn't know if I could soberly cross this line. I searched his eyes looking for a sign so that I could run away and forget this happened. His dark blue eyes kept drawing me into him. I can't believe this is happening.

I felt a sharp pain go through my head again, and I wanted to fall on the floor, but it was like a warning. I took it and went into the bathroom getting in the shower. Usually, I wouldn't be so irresponsible to sleep with my boss. My mind began to race and pieces of the night flashed before me. I can't believe this happened.

I sat at the bar watching my best friend Reign dancing with her husband Brenton and tossed back the rest of the Gentleman's Jack in my glass. I was overjoyed for her. She had found love, gotten married, and will live happily ever after. As much as I wanted that luxury of doing that, I couldn't. My past was too muddy to bring anyone else into it. I already had broken the rules when Reign and I became friends, I couldn't bring a husband in this life too. I raised my hand to get the bartenders attention. Once he walked over to me, I tapped the glass in front of me for another round. Once it was refilled, I tossed it back and tapped the glass again before the bartender walked off.

"Why are you over here sulking?" Dennis' familiar baritone voice came from behind me. He came sitting behind me taking me in with the bluest eyes I have ever seen in my life.

"I'm not sulking. I'm celebrating our best friends' happily ever after." I lifted my glass in the air.

"To the bride and groom." Dennis lifted his glass in the air, and that was the first of many toasts that I shared with him last night.

CPSIA information can be obtained
at www.ICGtesting.com
Printed in the USA
LVHW031910080319
610001LV00001B/125/P